FINDING
❧ FAITH ❧

TRISHA KOOP ABEAR

DRL
press

Hardcover ISBN: 979-8-9893033-6-6

Soft Cover ISBN: 979-8-9893033-7-3

DRL Press, Georgetown, Texas

Design and Production: Riverstone Group, LLC

CONTENTS

PROLOGUE

After signing his name several times, on two very different sets of documents, Samuel felt closure for one chapter and a new breath of hope for the next. He knew he still had a number of months before his term was up and his letter of request still needed approval, but he had given twenty years of his life to the United States military and after much thinking, he had made some big decisions. He was excited to return for good to Maggie and his home in Crosby, Minnesota.

Lacing his boots up tight and pulling his hat on snug he took a last glance in the cloudy mirror that hung next to a cross he had brought months ago when his deployment to Afghanistan began.

He smiled, despite the danger he frequently was in here. His thoughts were on Maggie. Beautiful Maggie. He wondered if she was thinking of him at this very moment too. He longed to cuddle next to her in their bed at home that she always kept soft and cozy with flannel sheets and a down comforter. It was never easy waking up in the morning. And with her in his arms, he sometimes was tempted to call in sick. He missed her terribly, but now he saw the light at the end of the tunnel.

He would turn in his papers immediately before he set out on a training mission with several other soldiers at 0800.

Both files in his hand were important, perhaps one even more than the other.

Samuel felt he was doing the right thing. He hoped Maggie would agree.

CHAPTER 1

ONE YEAR LATER

Maggie cracked two eggs into the hot cast iron skillet her mother had given her as a birthday gift years ago. She stared down at the sizzling white and yellow in the pan only seeing the blur of colors for a minute. She had been struggling with the memory of Samuel this week. There didn't have to be any major event that brought him into her mind, usually it was just a small thing. If she saw a young couple walking hand in hand down the sidewalk, she remembered their young years. If she noticed a soldier coming off the airplane hugging his family after many months apart, she lost her breath wishing that were her. This morning it was simply the fact that she was cooking herself fried eggs, and she knew Samuel would have asked for scrambled with cheese.

Oh Samuel. Could one soul be so perfect? He had always treated Maggie like a treasure he had been searching the world for. Of course they had little spats from time to time. Afterall, they were human. But somehow they always found a way to discuss things and come back to their main goal together- finding their dreams. Living out a wonderfully rich, wholesome life- with just a touch of adventure.

Maggie flipped her eggs. She was going for over-easy, but when she made eggs she always told the person she was serving them to, "ya get what ya get and don't throw a fit." That's what her mom had told Maggie and her siblings, although Mom's eggs always tasted perfect. Throwing two pieces of raisin bread into the toaster, she made a mental note to call mom this afternoon. Her mom, Sarah, would be having her coffee break and perhaps reading a book at 3:00. They could visit for a while.

Her eggs were perfectly cooked right as her pieces of toast popped up steaming hot. Maggie buttered the pieces and slid her eggs right on top. Samuel always said it was a weird breakfast, but Maggie told him "Don't knock it til you try it." She would wink and he would laugh while he scarfed down his cheesy eggs atop a toasted bagel she made special for him.

They'd sit at the kitchen table sipping coffee, enjoying their meal while looking out their front window at the pond. Usually in the spring the swans would return and glide across the blue waters. Loons would join soon after and an occasional Sandhill crane. Samuel would dress in his Army attire, kiss Maggie on the forehead and leave for work at Fort Jefferson. He worked there as a commanding officer and had served overseas three times since enlisting.

Maggie pushed her half-eaten plate of food away thinking back to his third deployment overseas. His last time. He had been taken from her on a Tuesday at 7:00 a.m. Had he been home with her, she would have been scooping his scrambled eggs onto his plate at that very minute. She had been living free, living life, not knowing where he was or what was happening to him. The truck he and his comrades were riding in the back of was blown to bits traveling through the deserts of Afghanistan. They were only traveling to another base, weren't even in combat and taken completely by surprise.

Samuel had been on several dangerous missions during his deployments, many of which he had led. Maggie shivered thinking to herself, *After all he had been through and sacrificed – what a senseless way to go.* But war was never pretty.

The officer that delivered the news to her had spared her the details, but said that it was confirmed the group was killed on contact. No suffering. At that moment Maggie remembered thinking, "I wish I had been with him, so that I may have avoided the suffering too."

As suffering and pain, for Maggie, came.

It had been a full year now since the worst day of her life. And ever so slowly she had been healing; coming back to the living. Rinsing her dishes, she placed them in the dishwasher and grabbed her keys and purse from the table by the front door. The store opened at 9:00 and she had never been one minute late flipping the open sign on her front door. She owned a small store on Main Street, Crosby called *The Maple Leaf*. She sold seasonal household decor and homemade goods made by locals.

Samuel had watched her work at various jobs for the first ten years they were married, knowing her dream had been to own her own little store on Main Street. A year before he left for his last deployment, this little building had come up for sale and he purchased it without even telling Maggie. He had even stuck a giant red bow on the front door when he brought her there. What a gift it had been. *The Maple Leaf* had been her lifeline after losing him.

The front door bells jingled above as she unlocked it and stepped inside. She flipped her little sign showing through the window glass to 'Open' and walked back to the checkout counter. Maggie flipped the light switch on and the room illuminated. She fiddled with her cordless speaker and connected it to her playlist. The soft comforting music she always played started with the smooth voice of Nat King Cole. She lit one of her apple scented candles on the counter to lend to the mood of crisp fall air creeping into Minnesota. Stores like *The Maple Leaf* always had brought her warm, cozy feelings of home. She had always aspired to own a shop that gave those who visited it the same feelings. And now it was her reality.

Needing another cup of coffee (or maybe just the warm feeling of it in her hand), Maggie poured coffee grounds into her coffee maker and pushed the 'brew' button. Soon, the rich smell filled the room. She busied herself unpacking boxes with new items to stock her shelves.

October was in full swing and the colors of bronze, crimson and warm oranges filled her store. Leafy garland hung above the front window with twinkling lights entwined. She had primitive, wooden pumpkins and black wooden crows to stick on a fence post or deck railing. Distressed white hutches were pressed against the wall displaying seasonal candles on the shelves, like the apple scented one Maggie was burning today.

A few black farmhouse tables and chairs were scattered here and there with full place settings atop them. Maggie hung Billy Jacobs's paintings on her walls; her favorite artist. His work was of simplicity, but of the most appealing kind. Maybe her shoppers didn't always feel the emotions she did when looking at his classic works like "Stone Cottage" which hung on the wall in her living room at home. At any rate, *The Maple Leaf* had been a labor of love and had become a success in town.

Maggie heard the front door bells ring as she was ripping the packing tape off another cardboard box filled with table runners. She walked out front to find fellow shop owner, Mabel, holding a warm slice of pecan pie wrapped tightly with cellophane. Mabel owned the bakery, *Pumpernickel House*, with her husband Henry and had for many years, in Crosby. Though most people traveling through town figured the name of the bakery came from the wonderful tasting bread called Pumpernickel Rye, Pumpernickel was actually the couple's last name. Mabel said they knew they were destined to own a bakery someday.

"Mabel, come on in! How about a quick cup of coffee?" Maggie suggested while pulling out a chair at one of her beautifully decorated tables.

"No, no honey. I've got pans of popovers that are needing to be pulled out in five minutes and counting. Just wanted to bring you a fresh piece of pecan pie. I know it's your favorite!" Mabel said, handing the plate of the sticky, warm dessert to Maggie.

"Awww, you remembered? Well, thank you Mabel. I am going to sit down in a bit and enjoy this with my coffee." Mabel and Maggie visited for only a minute or two before Mabel said she had to be off.

Maggie brought the plate to the back room and sat it down by the coffee maker. Just one taste and then back to work. She grabbed a fork and pulled the cellophane from the pie. Steam swirled up to her nose and the sweet, nutty, comforting smell made Maggie close her eyes and smile, remembering holidays gone by. She sliced a small bite off with her fork and took a taste. MMMMM, better than she remembered. Sugary, roasted nuts swimming in a gooey filling and a flaky pie crust that only could indicate it was made with pure lard. Oh, but such a splurge was worth it!

Maggie took one more bite while she reminisced back to the day her mother had taught her to make her first pie. Carefully they would cut the shortening and flour with the pastry cutter and stir in water; cold water. They would dust the pastry cloth with a handful of flour and roll out the delicate pie dough with their rolling pins. Pie brought Maggie back to her childhood, the carefree days. Her childhood was a very sheltered one, a very wholesome one. She was thankful of it, but had she been prepared for the pains life throws at you? No. But, maybe nothing could have "prepared" her for the pain of losing her soulmate. Nor the tragedy that had taken him from her.

Wrapping up the remaining pie, Maggie set it aside and went back to her work. Life happens. There's no way around it. Best to make yourself busy and keep looking forward.

Nothing could heal the past.

CHAPTER 2

Rose rocked Jade to sleep while Sophia was tucked snuggly on Flynn's chest as he laid back on the arm chair. The couple had new twin baby girls August 19th and the first weeks had been a real challenge. They could not love two tiny humans more than they did Jade and Sophia, but a few consistent hours of sleep would be amazing. To Rose's relief, her mother Evie had come to help out for the first days, but now it was Flynn and her on their own. And Flynn was needed back at Fort Jefferson ten days from today. Rose wasn't really looking forward to him leaving. She was new at this; being a mom. And two babies at once? How about when she reopened the Inn again? And guests started coming? Thank God she had hired Lucille to help in the kitchen and Marie to clean rooms and wash linens a few days a week.

Rose stroked Jade's silk smooth black hair matted on her sweaty little head. She breathed in the lavender scent of baby shampoo that still lingered from the bath she had that evening. Her yellow baby blanket was swaddling her tight and finally the content breaths of sleep could be heard from her pink little lips as Rose brought her to her bassinet. Walking over to Flynn, she scooped up Sophia and tucking her in close, Rose wrapped her pink blanket tightly around her sleeping body. She softly kissed her chubby little cheek and set her down for a night's rest in the bassinet next to her sister's.

Rose tugged on Flynn's shirt and motioned to the bedroom for a more comfortable place to sleep. Her husband stumbled after her. On autopilot the two dressed in their pajamas and crawled into their antique four post bed. Rose pulled the quilt up to their chins and curled up against her husband. "Thank you for being the best husband and daddy in the world," she whispered softly in his ear. She heard a soft snore and it made her smile.

As tired, exhausted really, as Rose was she couldn't help thinking back on the last year. Flynn being deployed. Her car accident. Her unexplainable time in Cherish. Her coma. Finding out she was pregnant soon after. Moving and buying their Inn, *Simpler Times*. The list went on. Things were moving so fast in their lives and had been since the day the two had met. Rose had been working at the Canal Park Diner and Flynn came in. He had remembered an embarrassing event months before where Rose had spilled a milkshake on his lap. He hadn't really meant to come back to embarrass her with the memory. He had wanted to formally meet the cute waitress that had done so. They had shared a laugh about the instance and one thing led to another. Rose and Flynn had met, fell in love and were married in less than four months. It was an absolute whirlwind. Though all that they had done together since the day they met felt right. Exactly as it should be. Rolling onto her back she folded her hands and said a short prayer of thanksgiving. For her husband, her family, her perfectly beautiful babies and the Inn they owned and ran. She was wrapped a thousand times over in blessings and her heart was full.

After a few minutes Rose finally drifted off to sleep. After four hours, her breasts felt full and she looked at the clock. *Wow, this is a record.* Rose laid in her bed staring at the clock. After it ticked on for ten minutes she finally heard a tiny, hungry cry. And then another. Yawning, she smiled to herself. *Be patient mama, someday these babies will be grown up and you won't care that you missed a little sleep.*

CHAPTER 3

Opening the front door to Nora's coffee shop Maggie inhaled the scent of strong espresso and toasted bagels. There was a line at the counter, as usual, for everyone's favorite morning caffeine fix. Usually Maggie had a cup or two at home, or made a pot at the shop. But once in a while it was fun to sip on a Pumpkin Spice Latte while she walked down the sidewalk taking in the cool air, the cinnamon steam rising from her foam cup.

When she reached the front of the line she was greeted by Nora, the owner of *Cream and Sugar*. "Maggie, good morning! Haven't seen you come in for a while. Although, it is October now and I know you love the Pumpkin Spice Lattes."

Maggie laughed, "You know me very well, Nora. I've been meaning to walk down. Just busy I guess. How's it been going here? Busy?"

"Very. As you can see," Nora remarked, pointing to the people packed in the small shop.

"I do see. Well, that's a good thing right? Let me place my order so I can get out of your hair. As you guessed, I will have a tall Pumpkin Spice and I would also like one of your Everything Bagels to go, please."

After paying Nora and grabbing her breakfast, Maggie waved goodbye to her friend. Nora had owned *Cream and Sugar* longer than Maggie had owned *The Maple Leaf*. There had been many times through the years that the two had shared advice about this and that and tried to promote each other's businesses. It had also been nice to have a friend after Samuel had passed away. Nora, along with many of the shop owners in town, had offered to do anything they could for Maggie. The truth was, there was nothing. She plain and simply needed time. And even with that it had been a year she wouldn't wish on her worst enemy.

Maggie walked down the sidewalk toward her shop and took a small sip of her sweet drink. If this warm liquid wasn't the taste of Autumn, then she didn't know what was.

She savored each tiny sip as she slowly took her time down Main Street. She glanced down to the end of 3rd Street on her way, noticing the two-story yellow and white house that had recently been opened as an Inn. The sign out front read, *Simpler Times*, a name that fit perfectly.

Maggie hadn't met the new owners just yet, but she sure had admired what they had done with the old house. It had sat at the end of 3rd Street for years, waiting for the right buyer to come along. This couple had a vision in their minds of exactly what they wanted and went for it. Maggie admired that. Still peering down at the Inn and not paying attention to what was in front of her, she bumped right into a large, solid man, tipping her latte down the front of her sweater.

"Oh my goodness! I'm so sorry sir...Clem? Oh, Clem. I must be daydreaming this morning. I didn't even see you there," Maggie apologized, wiping her sweater off with a napkin she had tucked in the bag with her bagel.

"Maggie? You didn't see *me*? I'm hard to miss!" Clem teased.

Clem owned *Clem's Groceries*. He was a big guy. A big black guy. Intimidating to see walking down the sidewalk, but had the heart of a little teddy bear. He reminded Maggie of Michael Clarke Duncan, the actor who famously starred in the movie *The Green Mile*. Clem was probably sixty years old and still towered at 6 ft 3in, 280 pounds. Maggie couldn't imagine him at twenty-five years of age. Maybe he was someone's bodyguard back then. She sure would've hired him had she been a Mariah Carey or Celine Dion back in the day.

"Very funny Clem. Yes, well, I should've been paying attention. It's my own fault I have half my latte down the front of my sweater now. A *white* sweater no less," Maggie groaned trying to move her plaid scarf to cover the tan stain. The two friends looked at each other and started to laugh. Clem put a hand on Maggie's shoulder and said, "Ahh, sis, ya can't cry over spilled milk... or in your case, coffee."

"Right you are Clem. At least I still have half a cup to enjoy back at the shop," she replied.

"That a girl," Clem said, waving her on her way. He said it to her in a way a father would tell his daughter when she was moving on, when she was being strong, when he was proud of her. Clem had loved Samuel and knew that Maggie did more than anyone. But he wanted her to be happy again...Someday.

After collecting herself, Maggie found a garbage can on the next block corner and threw away her soiled napkins and turned down 3rd Street. She sipped the remaining latte which was surprisingly still warm. She didn't intend to spy, but she wanted a closer look at *Simpler Times*. The two story home had sat at the end of this lonely street for years. Maggie found herself wondering if it had been haunted. It was a turn of the century two story Victorian. She pictured perhaps the mayor of Crosby and his family lived there in the 1920s or maybe it had been an Inn even back then. Either way, this new couple, the Mitchells, from what she had heard, had given new life to the house.

Maggie shuffled along the sidewalk, getting closer, sipping her coffee casually. The wooden sign in the front yard was painted white and someone with artsy skill had scrolled the words *Welcome to Simpler Times*. Hard work had constructed the matching white picket fence surrounding a now browning garden. Still, crimson mums were potted down the walkway and placed on the front steps which led to a covered porch. Two orange pumpkins sat on both sides of a very large front door made of solid oak. Maggie didn't realize she had stopped and was picturing happy guests or family members swaying back and forth on the bench swing as they sipped cider and laughed happily together.

"Oh, can I help you?"

This time the remains of Maggie's latte flew up in the air as she gasped, startled by the stranger's voice.

"Oh my goodness. I'm sorry. I didn't mean to scare you. And look, your coffee is creating rivers in the sidewalk cracks. Come on in, I will give you a fresh cup." the nice young lady offered.

"I didn't mean to stand in front of your Inn and stare, but I was admiring the work you've done. It is lovely!" Maggie complemented. "I mean, I assume you're the owner? Mrs. Mitchell is it?"

"Rose. Yes, well this Inn was my dream. My husband, Flynn, helped me make it a reality. It's been a labor of love, most definitely, but it has been my joy also." Rose looked at the yellow and white house with a proud smile and then turned back to Maggie.

"But, please come on in for a moment if you are able. I just finished brewing a fresh pot of coffee and the cranberry bread is just about ready to come out of the oven."

Rose led Maggie up the front steps and opened the door for her.

"Well, thank you, Rose. I am Maggie, by the way. I own *The Maple Leaf* on Main Street, right next to *Pumpernickel House*." Maggie replied.

"Oh, I will have to come check out your store. I'm sorry, we haven't been to all the great shops in town since opening *Simpler Times*, but I am going to add that to my list of places to stop by." Rose told Maggie.

As the two women stepped inside, the warm, comforting feeling of home surrounded Maggie. There was a light smell of sweet bread baking in the kitchen and the crackling sound of logs burning in the fireplace. October was beginning to produce a few occasional cold days and the scent gave a cozy feeling.

"I love your decorating style, Rose." Maggie remarked as she sat down on an oversized armchair. "*The Maple Leaf* is a home decor store so I notice these things."

Rose appeared excited with this news. "Another one of my passions is choosing new pieces to grace my living room and front porch. And yet *another* reason why I need to visit your shop, Maggie."

As Rose excused herself to the kitchen Maggie sat by the fire and further studied the special touches of Rose's Inn. Maggie thought she was somewhat of an expert on home decor, but Rose's taste had such an old fashioned, yet classic, style. Maggie almost couldn't categorize her taste. She noticed the fine details.

Accompanying the large wingback arm chair Maggie sat in was a matching emerald green chair, also facing the fireplace. On the small table between the chairs sat only a single wrought iron candlestick holder with a beeswax candle in place. But then, on a small shelf near the foyer, was a framed picture of a little girl with her arms around a man and a woman, probably her parents, dressed as Dorothy from the wizard of Oz. Her mother and father proudly dressed as the scarecrow and the wicked witch. The Inn was beautifully and classically presented, but also held the coziness of a childhood home. Maggie felt a comfort she hadn't felt for some time. Strange how the two styles could coincide so well. Clearly something Rose had a knack for organically. You wouldn't see this in an Interior Decor magazine.

Moments later Rose came back into the room with a tray. On it sat a China teacup on a matching saucer next to a creamer pitcher and a dish of sugar cubes. Also, on a separate plate was a fresh slice of cranberry walnut bread with a pat of butter melting into the spongy delicacy. Rose set the tray on the black colonial style table next to Maggie and took the seat across from her.

"Please Maggie, help yourself. My husband claims my cranberry walnut bread is award winning, but I don't know." Rose said shyly.

"Oh thank you. This looks wonderful!"

After sipping her coffee and sampling the warm bread, Maggie began,

"I think your husband is right. This bread is absolutely to die for!"

Rose cordially smiled and nodded. "It's so nice to meet you Maggie. Flynn and I have been hoping to meet more people from this lovely town of Crosby. Flynn is my husband. He is in the Army Reserves and works at Fort Jefferson."

Maggie froze. Her hand holding the priceless teacup, probably a gift from Rose's great great grandmother, started to shake. Feeling a bead of sweat start forming on her brow, she decided to set it down on the tray.

Rose noticed immediately the way Maggie had responded, but didn't want to make her feel uncomfortable.

"Now that he is back to work, I have all I can do to manage this place and the babies on my own."

Maggie's demeanor changed and she was glad of the change of subject.

"Babies? You run an Inn, cook and bake award winning dishes AND care for twins?" Maggie mused.

Rose smiled, replying, "Yes, Jade and Sophia are napping at the moment. They still take two long naps a day and so that is when I get things done around here!"

"Awww, two little girls huh? What a blessing." Maggie meant it, but forced a genuine, albeit envious, smile. "I'm going to let you get back to it, Rose. I really appreciate you inviting me into your home, your Inn, this morning. I hope that we will see each other again."

As if on cue, a tiny cry came from up the stairs. Both women looked in that direction and smiled.

"I guess that is my cue to get back to work." Rose giggled. "And my pleasure, Maggie. We will definitely be making a trip to *The Maple Leaf* soon."

Maggie waved goodbye to a new friend, perhaps one she could share stories and tears with, being Rose's husband was also a US soldier. He may have even served overseas. Maybe even in Afghanistan like Samuel.

Maggie felt a tightness in her chest and a sting in her stomach. She didn't know if she yearned for such a friend or wanted to run from one.

With the crisp, cool air coating her lungs, she picked up the pace. *The Maple Leaf* opened at 9:00 and it was a quarter til.

CHAPTER 4

"I can't decide Maggie. Do you like the checkered black and white or the checkered orange and white," Mrs. Given asked, while looking at the new table runners. "The black and white would work so well with my kitchen, but I like the orange and white for the Autumn season."

Mrs. Given lifted each in her hand, laid the woven runners on the display table as if it was her own, folded them and unfolded them. One might think she was deciding on which material to use for the queen's ball gown. But Maggie sweetly smiled, the creases in her cheeks forming. She loved seeing a customer come into her shop and fall in love with pieces. Pieces that would grace their home. The place they made memories. The place they cried, they laughed, they reminisced. And Mrs. Given was no exception. Maggie could tell Mrs. Given was picturing just the perfect table runner for her usual Thanksgiving dinner coming soon. A trivial detail? Not for Mrs. Given. And that's what Maggie loved about owning *The Maple Leaf*.

"Sylvia, let's look at each table runner spread out on my oval table. I will grab some white dinner plates and set them at each place setting and let's center some oversized pillar candles in the middle of the table to get a formal feel. How does that sound?" Maggie suggested.

"Oh, my dear girl, you are good at what you do," Mrs. Given replied and began rearranging the table.

The bells of the shop door jingled as it was opened. Mrs. Given and Maggie looked up from their task. Maggie was pleased to see Rose pushing a stroller with two sweet little baby girls riding inside, both bundled up for their fall walk through town.

"Rose, I'm so happy you finally made the trip over. And I'm equally excited to meet your twins." Maggie greeted them. "Mrs. Given, please excuse me. Take your time deciding though. No rush at all."

Maggie walked over to Rose and her little ones.

"Maggie! I have been making plans to come visit for the last two weeks and things came up at the last minute. Jade had a cough, I suddenly had double the rooms booked, and Lucille took a few days off." Rose waved her hands in the air. "But no more excuses. Show me around!"

"Of course. Let me take a peek at these little cherubs first," Maggie exclaimed.

Folding the soft pink blanket back she saw a perfectly round little face, long eyelashes and a sweet pouty mouth. Maggie did the same to her twin, and her face couldn't hide the envious admiration.

"They are such dolls, Rose. You and Flynn are blessed. Truly."

Rose, too, gazed down at her daughters. It was obvious they were her sheer pride and joy.

"Thank you. Aside from Jade's habit of wanting to be wide awake at 3:00 a.m. lately and Sophia's frequent spit ups, they are angels." Rose winked at Maggie and the two began a mini tour of Maggie's shop.

"What a lovely hutch, Maggie. I have been searching for one for my dining room. I may have to have Flynn come take a look with me. This one would look beautiful in *Simpler Times*." Rose said, studying the lovely solid piece of furniture.

"It certainly would. By the way Rose, I have been wanting to tell you what a wonderful thing you and Flynn did with that old house. I could have cried a million tears seeing the years go by and that diamond in the rough sitting dark and vacant. It is a joy, really, to see what you have made of it. I knew eventually a special someone would bring it back to life." Maggie added.

Rose's eyes appeared to moisten at the incredible compliment.

"Oh, Maggie. You have no idea of the road that brought us to *Simpler Times*. Someday, maybe you and I will sit with a warm cup of coffee and I will share the story with you. In short, it has been a dream come true."

"Maggie dear. I have finally decided." Mrs. Given announced from the front counter. Maggie turned. "I'll be right up, Mrs. Given."

"Thanks for stopping in, Rose. Bring Flynn by any time to take a closer look at the hutch." Maggie winked.

"Ha. I will do that. Maybe I'll serve his favorite Pan-fried Walleye with Wild rice and Brussel sprouts before we stop in. He'll be in an extra happy mood."

The two laughed as Rose pushed the stroller out the front door and continued down the sidewalk.

"Ok, Mrs. Given. What did we decide?"

CHAPTER 5

Maggie laid awake. She had slept for a few hours, but her Zzzquil pills could only work for so long it seemed. Every night was different and extremely unique in the reasoning for her insomnia. Tonight it was a thought (a relentless thought) of what her and Samuel's babies may have looked like. That thought made her think of if they might have had a girl or a boy. What would they have named their baby? But things always came back to, Why? Why weren't they able to conceive? Why didn't they have more time? Why did he have to die before they had come up with a plan? LIFE! Sometimes Maggie became tired. No, not just tired, but the extreme definition of exhausted. Life without Samuel and without any hope of their child being brought into this world was enough to make her just want to lay down and die. And yet, even sleep, of all things, wouldn't give her the satisfaction of indulgence.

Somehow her 2:00 a.m. thoughts switched gears to her newfound friendship with Rose Mitchell. She seemed to be a very kind, down to earth, relatable woman. Though a good decade younger than Maggie, she felt a connection with Rose. Perhaps, if nothing else, it was that they both had been married to military men. Soldiers who had served overseas. Plus, on a much less dramatic scale, their appreciation for new recipes and vintage home decor seemed to be a common likeness and a frequent topic of conversation between the two.

Maggie had been invited on occasion to *Simpler Times* for coffee on the porch or to take a stroll around town with Rose and the twins. Maggie learned that the couple had moved to Crosby from Duluth in hopes of finding a fixer upper home that would be perfect for an Inn, during which time plans changed and Flynn was deployed.

Maggie realized Samuel would have been stationed in Afghanistan around the same time Flynn had been. Only Flynn had returned and Samuel had not. Typically Rose would change the subject if their conversations slid in the direction of Flynn's time overseas. She could tell that Maggie carried deep scars, still, from the pain she suffered only one year ago.

Maggie laid on her down pillow staring into the darkness above her, thinking. Once she realized she was mentally making a note of what deliveries were coming into the shop in the morning, pondering what the theme of her senior prom had been and whether she preferred oatmeal or cereal more, she accepted that the task of forcing sleep on herself was useless. Flipping the fluffy down comforter off her legs she yawned and got to her feet. It was now 4 a.m. and still pitch black outside.

"Coffee time," she announced to the empty kitchen as she reached into the cupboard for the coffee canister.

Within minutes the rich smell of freshly brewed coffee filled the room. When Maggie breathed in deeply, it reminded her of the Folgers commercials. She smiled despite the restless night she had experienced. Afterall, it wasn't an unusual occurrence. She had begun to recover pretty quickly and move on with her days.

Sipping her steaming cup of coffee, Maggie looked at her wall calendar. Halloween was this Friday. She needed to decorate the shop and buy some candy for the trick or treaters. There were always lots of kids parading down the sidewalks of Main Street on Halloween evening. Little ghosts dressed in white sheets their mom had thought of at the last minute when she had forgotten to buy a costume. Little boys dressed up as Luke Skywalker or Batman. Little girls as princesses or witches. Maggie looked forward to the holidays. Halloween kind of kicked off the season. After a quick bowl of cornflakes, Maggie went upstairs to hop in the shower. "If I'm up this early, I may as well start the day and do something productive."

CHAPTER 6

Rose was sweeping the front steps when she saw Maggie pull up in her white Jeep Cherokee. Waving, she walked over to where Maggie had parked.

"Hi, Maggie. You're up and at 'em this morning." Rose greeted her. Maggie rolled her eyes and laughed. "Yes, well when I finally realized I had laid awake in my bed long enough to have watched the entire movie *Titanic*, I decided it was time to give up and start the day."

Rose giggled. "Well, do you have time to come in for a quick cup of coffee or some peppermint tea?"

"Sure, I could for a few minutes. The reason I stopped by was to let you take a look at these swatches you were interested in for the drapes your husband doesn't know you're ordering."

"Shhhhh, he's right in the kitchen." Rose teased as they walked through the front door. "Honey, don't leave just yet, I want you to meet Maggie, finally." Rose opened the swinging kitchen door for Maggie and like a gentleman, Flynn stood up from his chair and held out his hand.

"Maggie, I've heard a lot about you. I'm glad we are finally able to meet. Rose tells me your husband was in the Army also?"

Maggie shook Flynn's hand and answered, "Yes, that's right. Samuel had been, coincidentally, deployed to Afghanistan about the same time you were there I imagine. He died a little over a year ago while there."

No matter how many times Maggie said that sentence, she still had yet to do so without her bottom lip quivering.

"I'm sorry for your loss, Maggie. I, as his brother-in-arms, am in his debt for making the ultimate sacrifice." Flynn nodded at Maggie with respect and then switched gears. "Well, it was wonderful meeting you Maggie, but I need to shove off. I have to do a hundred pushups if I'm late again."

Maggie was happy with the way Flynn lightened the mood so quickly making her feel comfortable.

"Bye sweetie. Have a great day." Rose gave Flynn a quick kiss and he shut the front door behind him.

"Sit, Maggie, please. I'll pour you a cup of coffee and we can study these swatches."

Maggie pulled out the antique wooden chair and sat down. She thumbed through the swatches of colorful material herself until Rose joined her. Sipping on hot coffee, the two looked through each swatch pondering which would look best amongst Rose's furniture and general color scheme of the Inn.

"I like this burgundy color don't you, Maggie?" Rose suggested.

"Yes, that is the one I am picturing too." Maggie responded.

"Let's go with it then. If we are both in agreement, then it must be perfect." Rose smiled and took a satisfied sip of coffee. Setting her cup back on the saucer, she looked at the time.

"I better check on the girls. They were both up at 5:00 a.m. for a feeding, but it's nearly 8:00 now. Those little turkeys are sleeping in today."

Maggie laughed. "You go ahead, Rose. I need to get the shop open anyway. I will put in the order for your drapes. It shouldn't take but a week to have them in. I will let you know." She set her cup and saucer on the counter and turned to leave.

"Thanks again for the coffee. We'll talk soon."

"Sounds good, Maggie. See you later."

Maggie stopped at the post office before deciding to take the long way through town. Not in a hurry to open *The Maple Leaf* today, she decided to drive and admire the morning bustle of the town. Big yellow school buses were traveling down Main Street and turning on to 2nd Ave toward the elementary school, students piled cozily in the seats inside. She drove past *Clem's* and noticed he was flipping his window sign to Open. Down another block she saw Stuart Vontrapp, who owned his own dental office, walking away from *Cream and Sugar* with a large Cappuccino in hand. No doubt his fuel to keep his patience while dealing with whining "patients" throughout the day. Caroline, the town gossip, was rushing out the door of the coffee house just behind Stuart. It was clear to everyone in Crosby she hoped to become Mrs. Vontrapp, though Stuart gave her not a glimpse of a chance. It was peculiar really. Caroline was beautiful. She had shiny black hair that flowed like that of a Disney princess, unreal and animated almost. She smiled a white toothy grin complete with perfectly glossed lips. Her body was fit, but curvy- plump where it counted. But Stuart had no interest. Clem told Maggie, "The man is crazy. Caroline is an angel granting a troll a chance." Maggie had always punched Clem's oversized arm when he made the comment. Though, she knew Stuart had integrity. It had to take a lot of willpower and courage to shun Caroline given her sex appeal, but she was shallow, petty and well, frankly, you don't get the nickname of the town gossip by being a kind and loyal friend to the business owners on Main Street. She was playing for Caroline and Caroline only.

Maggie shook her head watching Caroline speed up her stiletto clad cadence to reach Stuart. Ahhh, you had to give the woman some credit. She just never gave up.

Finally, parking at *The Maple Leaf,* Maggie shut off her vehicle. It was quiet and dark as she pushed the back door open. Almost like a childhood home the smell and familiarity of the shop made Maggie feel comfortable and content. As she had said several times since Samuel's death, Thank God for *The Maple Leaf.*

Hanging her puffy Patagonia coat on the wall hook she, strangely, thought of the cat she had as a young girl. Cheddar was a snuggler. He loved curling up with her on her canopy bed and though Maggie now knew he didn't understand, at the time she would read him books, sing him songs and watch cartoons with him at her side, thinking he had enjoyed it. He was a big ole orange puff of a cat. Having lived for the major parts of Maggie's upbringing and being her best friend through thick and thin, it was hard letting him go—pet or family member. Maggie wondered why the thought of Cheddar just now, but the sudden idea to adopt a cat to make *The Maple Leaf* its home seemed like a great idea. A cat that was a few years old that would just roam the area and take naps on the chairs and under the tables. Maggie made a mental note to call HART and The Babinski Foundation to see what cats they had available for adoption.

She turned on all the lights making the room come to life. Every table, every chair, every shelf display, candle collection, kitchen towel, table runner and oven mitt set were still in their rightful place. As if on auto pilot, she went to the counter to turn on the mood music. Norah Jones was singing today. Maggie, out of habit, started the coffee maker and lit a few candles throughout the store. In her experience, women liked the cozy flicker of candles, but it was the scent of them burning- that made it almost impossible not to purchase at least one. Maggie, herself, couldn't deny the fact.

After lighting her favorite fall candle, the spicy scent of apple cider filled the room. Again a memory of long ago popped into her head…

She had taken Samuel with her to a local apple orchard, *Gilby's*. The fall day was perfectly cool, a light breeze sending yellow poplar leaves loose from their branches and onto the dirt paths surrounding the apple trees. Maggie was so excited for this day, she could hardly wait for the perfect moment. But she didn't want to ruin the surprise. She had it all planned out.

"So, Mags…you usually take your mom on this traditional fall excursion. Why me this time?" Samuel had asked on their drive.

"I don't know. I guess we just haven't gotten a whole lot of time together lately. I miss you," Maggie truthfully answered.

"Awww, that is so true. I'm sorry I've been so busy at work. Ya can't tell the US military you're sick of overtime," Samuel replied, attempting to make light of his heavy workload.

"Hey Hon. I'm proud of you. It's ok. Really, I just know you love my apple pie and I thought it extremely important you come and pick the apples this time. Don't you agree that is a must?" Maggie was trying to match his candor.

For the next few moments they both sat silent watching the road signs come and go as they got closer to *Gilby's*. Finally a large, brightly painted, wooden apple appeared in sight.

"Here we are!" Maggie announced.

Several people were milling around the orchard filling sacks with many varieties of apples—Granny Smith, Honeycrisp and Maggie's favorite, Golden Delicious. As Samuel pulled into the parking lot, Maggie noticed families enjoying the fun *Gilby's* offered. A dad helping his son and daughter pick just the right pumpkin for the transformation into their Halloween Jack-o-lantern. The mom nearby smiled as she bounced their baby brother in her arms. Children were like monkeys climbing on the giant hay bales that were set up and painted like Halloween characters- Frankenstein, a ghost and Darth Vador. Though Maggie didn't see the connection between Halloween and Darth Vador – she smiled at the beauty in front of her. It was all out of a novel, a dream, a lovely memory.

The bells on the front door of her shop interrupted her day dream. Maggie put the matchbox in her pocket and walked toward the front entrance to see who had just popped in.

"Stuart? Good morning. How are you today? Opening the office a bit later than usual today?" Maggie asked, surprised to see Dr. Vontrapp.

"Yes, the nine o'clock canceled and we don't have the root canal scheduled until ten." He cleared his throat, seeming to be a bit uncomfortable being there. Maggie couldn't recall ever seeing Stuart shop at *The Maple Leaf*.

"Oh, well that gives you time to kill I suppose. Can I help you find anything?" she offered.

"I, well, I am looking for a birthday gift for my sister. I am not great at picking out these sorts of things. I wondered if you would be of assistance perhaps? Maybe have an idea of what a thirty-five year old woman might enjoy?" Stuart fiddled with a package of coasters before deciding against it and looked up at Maggie.

Maggie chuckled. "I have been known to be good at picking out birthday gifts for women of all ages. Let's take a look."

Stuart seemed to relax and they turned left toward the apple scented candles that were perfuming the room with Autumn.

"I have yet to meet a woman who didn't enjoy getting a candle as a gift. These seasonal ones here in the mason jars are on sale." Maggie remarked picking one up to let Stuart see closer.

"Very nice. I will go with the Pumpkin Soufflé. What might go well as a filler? Could you put something together for me? I would pay extra?" Stuart looked down at his gray tennis shoes. "Really Maggie, I am not good at picking out gifts for women. Even my sister. So I would truly appreciate it."

Maggie laughed. "No problem at all Stuart. What price do you want to stay under?"

"Let's go with $100. I missed her last two birthdays, so I owe her."

"You got it. I have the perfect pairings in mind. Will you be picking it up after work today? I'm here until 5:00," Maggie told him.

"Yes, I will stop at about 4:00. Thanks again." Stuart smiled warmly and shut the front door behind him, the bells fastened to the handle jingling again. This was Maggie's favorite part about owning a home decor store. When someone entrusted her with the choosing of items she had hand-picked at market, she was suddenly inspired. Carefully, she chose a tightly woven wicker basket with a burlap liner. Carrying the basket in the bend of her arm she browsed her store as if she was a customer. Maggie placed the candle Stuart had chosen in the center of the basket. She folded a white flour sack kitchen towel next to it rolled tightly and bound with a crunchy string of raffia tied into a bow. Thinking of the candle, the towel and her favorite pastime when the cool air whistled through the trees on fall days, Maggie walked around the corner to where her recipe kits were displayed on a shelf made of barn wood. This basket needed a warm, inviting craving that could be made in minutes in anyone's oven. Caramel Oat scone mix was just the ticket. She placed the large bag with the mix, complete with directions printed on the back, into her basket. A few more things, she thought. After deciding on a set of red wine glasses and a bottle of locally made merlot, she felt the basket had come together perfectly. She was excited to show Stuart, though she had the feeling he wouldn't share the same enthusiasm she did. Ahh, well, Maggie certainly wasn't intrigued by tooth decay or the causes of gingivitis as he may be. Everyone had their place and purpose. And it was a good thing. She had learned years ago, her purpose was not exactly what she hoped it would be.

It caused a brief ache in her heart as the memory from earlier returned...

Samuel set down a large patchwork quilt in a clearing of grass between the rows of Gala apple trees. The couple sat down for a picnic lunch in the warmth of the sun, the smell of sweet fruit in the breeze. Maggie unpacked her basket she had carefully organized that morning. She handed Samuel a large mug and spoon and set down the same on the blanket for herself.

"What's for lunch today, Mags?" Samuel asked, anticipating something wonderful. Maggie loved to cook and according to her husband, she was the best at it.

"Nothing fancy today I'm afraid. You'll have to make do with it." Maggie replied with a wink. She pulled out a short insulated pot and twisted off the top letting steam rise carrying a tempting scent with it.

"Mmmmmm, you made my mom's steak chili didn't you?"

She smiled and poured the hearty dish into his mug. Samuel sat down comfortably crossing his legs, stirring his spoon in the chili.

"Don't take a bite until it cools down Samuel. You do it every time. Here, sprinkle a generous handful of shredded Colby jack on top to help the temperature come down faster," she said, handing him a small bag of cheese. Laughing to herself, she unpacked a loaf of rye bread, a couple bottles of water and two cloth napkins for her and Samuel.

"Maaaaggggiee, this is so good. How do you make it better each time?" He complimented her between bites. "Mmmmmm". Then swallowing, he asked, "So, what is the special occasion? You take me on an outing you've never invited me to and make my favorite chili? Something is up. I know it isn't our anniversary, or either of our birthdays. Come out with it, sneaky!"

Maggie smiled and sat next to him, kissed him softly on his smooth cheek and handed him an envelope.

"What is this? A large credit card bill you wanted to wait to show me until you buttered me up?" Samuel joked.

"No. This is something you will want to see. Something you maybe had lost hope in," she answered. Samuel looked closer and saw a joy in her bright green eyes he hadn't seen for some time and he knew.

"Maggie? Are you serious?" He asked while he pulled out the ultrasound photo. "Maggie, is this?" She nodded her head "yes" and he pulled her onto his lap hugging her tightly into his chest, no longer noticing his cup of favorite chili tipped over in the grass beside them. This was *the* day, the best day, a day they would never forget. They were going to have a family after all.

Maggie hadn't noticed a tear trickling down her cheek until the phone behind the counter rang. Shaking away the sad memories again, she wiped her cheeks, ran her hands through her dark hair and collected herself. After the third ring, Maggie answered with a forced cheer, "*The Maple Leaf,* how can I help you?"

CHAPTER 7

"Lucille, I'm off to do the shopping for the week, can you and Marie listen for the girls in case they wake up?" Rose asked as the sweet young lady she had hired a few months ago dusted the dining room light fixtures.

"Yes, of course Rose. We are happy to do so. They are such sweet little angels I would love the chance to hold them and play." Lucille laughed.

Rose smiled, "Yea, you wouldn't say that when Jade wakes up at 3:00 a.m. ready to play or Sophia has a temper tantrum because her breakfast is taking too long."

"This may be true." Lucille agreed. "Well, either way boss, be on your way. We will manage just fine here."

"I couldn't do it without you ladies!" Rose yelled as she strolled out the front door.

The fall air was becoming a bit more crisp as the season dwindled. Sometimes Rose could feel the slight hint of winter coming just around the corner. She craved a warm beverage to hold in her hand. She thought to herself, *Nora has some yummy Autumn favorites on special and well, why not?*

Pulling her Ford Focus in front of *Cream and Sugar* and putting it in park, she noticed Maggie's jeep was two cars ahead. "Yay Maggie. I haven't seen you in a while." Rose said out loud hoping her friend was in the coffee shop and they could visit for a few minutes.

As usual, the coffee shop was busy. Customers are never tired of caffeine, of sugar or of trendy new beverages. Coffee houses don't go out of style because they cater to all generations and all types of people. Rose was in agreement and she was happy for her new friend, Nora, who owned the shop. She was living her dream and running a successful business at the same time.

"Maggie! I'm so glad I caught you here. It's been a little while." Rose yelled when she saw Maggie, grabbing her in an embrace.

"Hi Rose. How are you?" Maggie answered. Rose felt a certain somberness she hadn't seen before. Did Maggie look tired or stressed or was there a sadness there she was trying hard to hide? Rose didn't know Maggie well enough just yet to wager a guess on which emotion was affecting her, but something wasn't just right.

"I'm good. Busy as can be. But I've been meaning to have you over for coffee or a glass of wine on the front porch. We are going to open the Inn again full time the week before Thanksgiving and I need your opinion on more window treatments." Rose tried to find a subject that Maggie usually got excited about. Nora handed Maggie her Pumpkin Latte and her cake donut.

"Thanks Nora. This looks great!" Maggie said to Nora and turned to leave. "Rose, that's a great idea. We should get together soon. I've got to run, quarter to nine and the shop is calling!"

"Oh, ok. That sounds good Maggie. Talk to you soon." Rose waved. Something wasn't ok with Maggie. Rose wondered if she just needed her space or did some poking and prodding need to be done. Rose admittedly was notorious for this. She was deep in thought when she realized Nora was speaking to her from behind the counter.

"Earth to Rose." Nora laughed. "What are you having today, Rose? You've been staring at the chalkboard menu above my head for five minutes, but something tells me you don't even see the words written."

"Oh, wow—I am sorry Nora. The girls didn't let me sleep much last night," Rose lied. The truth was, Jade and Sophia were finally sleeping through the night, 10-5, but she had to have some sort of excuse for her sudden trance.

"I am going to have the Toffee Swirl latte with oat milk, please." Rose finally decided, mostly because it was the first item she read.

"Good choice. I will have that up in a jiffy. You can sit, Rose. I'll bring it out to you." Nora offered. Rose smiled and found a table by the window. Her thoughts were still on Maggie's mood this morning. Was she missing Samuel more than usual? Was today an anniversary of some kind and the memories were flooding back? Who knows? Grief can come back and hit you like a sledgehammer at any given time she figured. For today, she made the decision to leave things alone. If she didn't hear from Maggie by Friday, for sure Rose was going to pay *The Maple Leaf* a visit. A friend is a friend. And if Maggie knew it or not, she may really need one right now.

CHAPTER 8

Friday came and Rose hadn't heard from Maggie. "Ok, girls, we are going to take a stroll to visit mommy's friend. Let's bundle you up for the outing," Rose announced to her baby daughters who were laying on the living room floor atop a large throw blanket. Jade was reaching with all her might to grab her tiny feet stretched into the air above her. Sophia held tight to a soft toy that looked like a giraffe and chewed on it until drool dripped down her pink chin. Both babies were happy and healthy girls. Flynn and Rose felt absolutely blessed. There were tired days and there were diaper blowouts. There was far less freedom and the work around the inn took twice as long to get done with the frequent interruptions. But, no other baby in the world was more loved and enjoyed than these two girls.

Rose proceeded to fasten a fuzzy bonnet around Sophia's chubby little face and did the same to Jade. After both were ready with warm sweaters and the tiniest leather booties on their feet, Rose sat them in their stroller and headed out the door.

November was just beginning, but the nip in the air made for a visible puff in front of her as she breathed. She walked briskly down the sidewalk until she reached *The Maple Leaf*. As she pushed open the large door with her backside, the bells above her rang telling Maggie she had a customer.

As usual the shop was perfectly decorated. I suppose if a person wanted to be successful owning a home decor store, they better be good at decorating their shop as well. The tables scattered here and there were taking on a new look of rustic Thanksgiving Day vibes. The large mahogany farm table in the center of the room was the most impressive. A massive glass hurricane lamp with three white pillar candles acted as centerpiece while an amber gold table runner stretched the length of the rectangle table from one end to the other. Sprigs of rosemary and branches of Eucalyptus leaves were laid atop the runner just right, Bittersweet adding a pop of orange here and there. To give the final feel of a family welcome to dine, Maggie had even set the table with perfectly classic white dinner plates and lovely glass stemware to hold a wonderful merlot or chardonnay to toast each other on Thanksgiving Day. Rose realized she had been staring at the sight for several minutes when Jade's giggle brought her back to the store.

Maggie was crouched down in front of the stroller playing peek-a-boo making both babies giddy with laughter.

"Oh, Maggie—I was in a trance admiring your table settings! You sure have a talent," Rose complimented. "I hope you will help me prepare my table for our Thanksgiving Day celebration. And we hope you will attend also. This is our first holiday celebration at the inn."

"That would be nice. And I would love to help you out, Rose." Maggie smiled politely. "I will have to check with my mother and see what plans she has for the day. She sometimes attends my aunt's outrageous parties, but she and I have also dined ourselves at her house with the comfort of old favorites."

"Oh, she would be absolutely welcome to come too," Rose replied.

"Thank you. I will extend the invitation when I talk to her this week," Maggie assured her. "So, is there something I can help you ladies with today? Looking for anything specific?"

Rose glanced around the room, wondering for a moment if she should make something up, as opposed to telling Maggie the real reason she ventured out for the visit this morning. After deciding that truth is the best avenue, she cleared her throat. "The truth is, Maggie, and maybe I'm out of line here, but as a friend of yours, I mean I feel like we are friends, well, I noticed at *Cream and Sugar*, and maybe I was imagining it…" Rose began to babble on.

"You saw a sadness in me?" Maggie finally offered.

Rose exhaled in relief. "Yes! I wasn't just imagining it? I thought maybe it was something I had said or done. I'm hoping not. Though I do want you to know I am here for you, if something is bothering you."

Maggie held Sophia's soft angelic hand in hers and rubbed it softly with her thumb. Without looking at Rose, she replied. "God has perfect plans for us all, I guess. On more than one occasion in my life, I have asked him what mine is. He has yet to give me a solid answer. I thought I was meant to be a loving wife and mother, but neither was the path He chose for me. Before I lost Samuel, I lost five babies too." Maggie's voice cracked and she stood up, no longer having the strength to look at such perfectly healthy babies smiling at her. Rose watched her friend. She looked tired. Maggie was such a naturally beautiful woman, but she looked older than her forty-two years. Grief and loss had aged her. Rose took her baby girls for granted, clearly. She sometimes even grumbled about them waking up multiple times in the night and spitting up for the fourth time in a row. But, my goodness, her and Flynn were so incredibly blessed to have little Jade Bean and Sophie Bear. They could truly not imagine life any longer without them. Rose's heart went out to Maggie. So much so that at that moment she felt her own eyes begin to well up with tears that threatened to trickle down her cheek.

"Maggie," Rose said as she softly grabbed her friend's hands in hers. "I am so sorry for your losses and the heartache you have had to endure these many years." Maggie looked away, not wanting to show emotion right away. Rose saw that she was uncomfortable, but continued. Someone had to be there for her. Whether Maggie was ready to open up or not, Rose was going to make sure it was very clear she was a shoulder she could cry on.

"Maggie, I don't know why God didn't choose such a soft hearted, nurturing woman to be a mother. But there is some purpose there. It is so hard to trust, as you know. But He is working His plan day by day through you. It will be revealed, but none of us know just when. Until then, let me be here for you. I won't pretend to know what you are going through, but I can listen." Rose embraced Maggie and then she finally crumbled. Tears fell and she let herself be weak for a rare moment.

The two finally retreated to the back room with the babies and Maggie made a fresh pot of coffee. Rose and Maggie visited for over an hour after Jade and Sophia each nursed and took a short nap in their stroller.

Finally, with puffy eyes and a much needed relief in her chest, Maggie waved to Rose as she pushed the stroller out the front door of *The Maple Leaf.*

On the walk back to *Simpler Times*, Rose had an unexpected emotion consuming her heart. Though she felt sadness for her friend, she felt such utter joy and gratitude for the babies in front of her. God had given her the gift of motherhood and she would never take it for granted again.

CHAPTER 9

"**M**rs. Pumpernickel, what a surprise. You've been so busy at the bakery. Please come in and have a seat," Maggie exclaimed, greeting her elderly friend.

"As usual, I brought you a treat, my sweet girl. It's getting to be lunch time though so I brought you a couple hearty slices of rye bread and Henry's homemade roast beef spread with red onion and sweet pickles. It's his specialty," Mabel said, proudly. Maggie smiled, genuinely. The Pumpernickels were the most thoughtful folks and they always treated Maggie almost like a daughter, being her mom lived a couple hours away now.

Leaning in for a soft hug, Maggie replied, "Ahhh, Mabel, thank you so much. This looks delicious. And Henry knows how I love his roast beef spread. Please give him my thanks also."

"I will do that, young lady. As usual I'm busy busy. A big order for our orange glazed sweet rolls came in this morning for the ladies brunch at Immanuel Lutheran church tomorrow. Henry can whip up a mean beef or ham spread, but the orange rolls are all this girl," Mabel said, pointing her thumb to her chest. Maggie waved out the shop door as Mabel walked slowly down the sidewalk to her quaint little bakery. The delectable scent, even from down the street, hovered in the air. Sweet, yeasty, warm fragrances— far better than any candle Maggie had in her shop. Henry and Mabel had owned and ran *Pumpernickels* for forty six years. Much of the building hadn't changed, aside from the few repairs and upkeep. The old tin ceiling, glass cabinets and old blackened ovens still graced the establishment. Mabel's mother's handwritten recipes hung in wooden frames and covered much of the wall where a few tables and chairs sat. In truth, Henry and Mabel were past retirement age, but much like old farmers who knew nothing but farming, they needed to keep the bakery running. They seemed to still love each day of work too. Maggie looked up to them.

Holding the blue China plate in one hand with two slices of brown bread and the container of the spread in the other, she decided now would be an excellent time for a break. In the back room she lathered a thick layer of spread on a piece of bread and took a big bite. "Mmmmmmm." Her great grandmother used to make the same spread from left over beef roast. She also added red onions and sweet pickles like in Henry's recipe. It tasted of when she was a young girl. Such happy times.

After finishing the last bite, she packaged up the remains and tucked them in her little fridge for tomorrow's lunch.

Since Rose's visit, Maggie had felt better. Of course the pain and memories would always be there, but every so often she needed to let the floodgates open and allow the emotional waters to rush. She didn't like to break down that way, but she felt so fortunate to have found a friend in Rose. And perhaps, spending time with her sweet baby girls could provide some healing rather than sorrow for Maggie. She still found sheer joy in seeing perfectly innocent little ones. Discovering the world around them, smiling at a stranger's face, being completely mesmerized by a simple leaf blowing in the breeze. After so many years, she still yearned for her own, but maybe God wanted her to be a friend, an occasional caretaker of babies instead. With all that Rose had to do at *Simpler Times*, she must need help from time to time with Jade and Sophia. Feeling a new, surprising burst of energy, Maggie decided she would offer her help to Rose and see what her and Flynn's thoughts would be. After the holiday season, she changed the open hours of *The Maple Leaf* to Wednesday thru Saturday 9:00-4:00. So, she would be available three days per week. And with Sundays being the busiest day at the Inn with check-outs, cleaning and prepping for the next week, Maggie guessed Rose and Flynn would be anxious for her help.

After adding up the money in her cash register and organizing the credit card receipts, Maggie flipped the sign on the front door to 'closed', switched the lights off and locked up. As she walked out into the dusky pink night clouds a sudden vision of Samuel's smiling face came to her. So real, so kind and such admiration in his dimpled smile. Maggie didn't feel sad. She felt comfort in seeing a quick fuzzy image of the man she still loved.

CHAPTER 10

Rose pulled the large salmon filet out of the oven, steaming with a light scent of dill and lemon filling the air while the perfectly cooked fish made her kitchen smell like a seafood restaurant. She breathed in the aromas as she set the tray on the stove top. Jade and Sophia sat nearby in their highchairs watching their mother's active dinner preparations.

"Ok, girls—what's next? I guess just steam the broccoli and slice a bit of this fresh oatmeal bread and we can call it a meal. For daddy and mommy anyway." The two smiley babies didn't understand what Rose was saying to them, but they didn't care in the least.

"Flynn, are you done in the shower? Dinner is ready!" Rose yelled up the stairs.

"Yep, Rosebud—I'll be down in a minute!" Flynn replied. Rose could hear his speedy footsteps down the stairs. Pushing the kitchen door open Flynn took a deep breath in just as Rose had done minutes before.

"Oooooh, it smells so good Rose. I love when you make salmon for dinner." Then noticing his daughters, Flynn's smile beamed. "My babies! Hi Jade Bean. How are you Sophie Bear?" The girls kicked their feet in excitement.

"Ok Hon, let's sit down to eat before the food gets cold, shall we?" Rose offered, pulling out both chairs at their simple kitchen table. The couple typically dined in the large dining room only when they were entertaining family or friends for the holidays and of course served their guests there.

Flynn filled his fork with flakey pink salmon and put it in his mouth, savoring the taste. Rose buttered him a slice of oatmeal bread and handed it over laughing. "Flynn, you act like you haven't eaten a thing all day."

"Ahh, it was busy today. I had a half a ham sandwich and a few pretzels, before being called away again." Flynn answered, grabbing the bread from Rose's hand. "Thank you, babe."

"Is there anything I should worry about? You won't be called back to Afghanistan so soon again I hope." Rose frowned and set her fork down, folding her napkin nervously in her hands instead.

Flynn reached over and took her fidgeting fingers in his large hands.

"Rosebud, please don't worry yourself. It is just busy work right now. And, though I may be deployed again, it will not be for at least a year. They have assured me of that." He reached up and tucked a loose strand of her blonde hair behind her ear and then tipped her chin up so she had to look him in the eyes.

"Look at me. It's ok. I'm here now," he attempted to sooth her sudden nerves.

As if the babies could sense their mom's tension, Sophia began to fuss. Rose wiped her mouth on her napkin and got up from her chair.

"Come here, Soph. It's ok." Feeling left out Jade started to whimper too.

"Oh, you silly girls. Here Rose, give me Sophia. She can sit on my knee while you grab Jade," Flynn offered and sat his pink pajama wearing daughter on his lap.

"You girls just want all the attention don't you?" Rose teased as she pulled Jade from her highchair. "Ok Flynn, we can each eat one handed can't we?"

The couple smiled at each other and as a family of four they finished their supper.

CHAPTER 11

Maggie hated going in for her semi-annual dental exam and cleaning. It felt good to have smooth shiny teeth and be given a thumbs up on her lack of cavities and general tooth decay, blah, blah, blah. But it just wasn't her favorite thing to do. And after canceling and rescheduling three times, she figured she better show up this time.

The same clean, freshly sanitized smell hit her when she walked into Dr. Vontrapp's dental office on Main Street. Lydia, seated behind the front counter, greeted Maggie cheerfully.

"Maggie! How are you? Do you have any more of those wonderful pumpkin muffin mixes left? I made a batch for Ken and the kids and they loooooooved them."

Maggie smiled, in spite of her sudden white coat syndrome causing an irrational anxiety.

"I am doing just great, Lydia. And yes, I do still have a few mixes at the shop. I'll hold a couple for you if you'd like. They are good. Have you tried the crème brûlée dessert dip mix? That one is a crowd pleaser too!"

"Ooooooo, set one of those aside for me as well," Lydia responded excitedly. Then, getting her head back to appointment scheduling, she looked at her computer.

"Ok, Maggie, It looks like we have your health history all up to date, unless anything needs to be changed?"

Maggie shook her head no.

"Then, you can take a seat. Stuart is running on time today, so should only be a few minutes. P.S.– don't tell him of the sugary treats we discussed. The man is always scolding us gals here about tooth decay."

"I heard that, Lydia." Dr. Vontrapp, Stuart, said as he walked up behind Lydia. Maggie laughed and Lydia rolled her eyes.

"Good morning, Maggie. I'm all ready for you. Come on back." Stuart led the way to his exam room. "Take a seat and make yourself comfortable. Katie will be in to do updated x-rays and your cleaning. But, I'll see you in a bit."

"That sounds great. Thanks Stuart."

After watching the clock tick by as Katie went about her work—buzzing, spraying, sucking, grinding, wiping," Maggie was relieved when she said, "Ok, all done Maggie. I will have Dr. Vontrapp come back to check things out."

Maggie sat waiting again. She thought about the gift basket she had made up for Stuart's sister's birthday and wondered if she had liked the present. As if on cue, Maggie heard the rolling stool squeak closer to her and Stuart appeared.

"Ok, Maggie. Any pain or concerns you have had lately?"

"Well, I wouldn't call it a concern really, but I was wondering if your sister liked her birthday present?" Maggie asked with a wink.

Laughing, Stuart answered, "She loved it. However, she didn't believe that I put together such a perfect basket of treats for her. Sooooo, I had to confess. But, it's not all bad news–she said she really wants to come check out your shop and she has a few good friends she knew would love to join her for a Saturday shopping spree. So, I'd say it was still a success."

"Good to hear. I'm happy to help with all your birthday shopping needs in future," Maggie replied. She almost felt relaxed with the easy conversation.

"Ok, let's take a quick peek shall we, Maggie? Then you can get out of here. Don't pretend you like sitting in this chair. I know you've canceled three times prior to today's appointment," Stuart accused in a teasing tone.

Maggie shrugged her shoulders pretending she had no idea what he was referring to.

After her exam, Maggie was given a thumbs up. Dr. Vontrapp gave her a small bag with the traditional toothbrush, toothpaste and floss.

"You're good to go, Maggie. Have a wonderful day. I'm sure I'll be needing more shopping assistance soon. My mother's birthday is next."

"That sounds great. Happy to help." Maggie shook Stuart's hand, walked past the front counter waving to Lydia and headed down the sidewalk for *The Maple Leaf.* She felt chipper today. It felt good. She finally got her nagging dentist appointment out of the way. She had a new order come in yesterday at the shop and she was anxious to start setting up the remaining Thanksgiving Day decorations, serving dishes and table cloths. Before long the season would transition to winter and Christmas. Remembering Thanksgiving Day fast approaching she figured she'd better stop by *Simpler Times* and talk to Rose about dinner plans. Her mother, Sarah, had decided to come and join Maggie for the occasion. Maggie was excited to introduce some of her friends to her mother. Since Dad passed away three years ago, Mom had kept to herself mostly. At first Maggie tried to push her to make friends, get out, find new hobbies. Sarah needed to do so in her own time. And slowly but surely, she did. She would call up Maggie and tell her of a women's luncheon she was attending or a book club she had joined with her friend, Gail. Maggie had felt better when her mother was finally able to live life on her own. After a couple is together for so long, losing them feels like losing one of your limbs. Painful and without a clue of how to function normally. Things were not easy at first. But Sarah was doing well now.

Maggie pulled her cell phone from her purse as soon as she got into *The Maple Leaf,* not wanting to forget to call Rose when she started getting too busy.

"Hello?" Rose answered.

"Hi, Rose! I thought I better give you a quick call about next week's big event and see if the invitation to have my mother join us still stands." Maggie said hopefully.

"Yes, of course! We would love to meet her. We are going to have a full house that day. A few friends from town that aren't able to be with their families that day will be joining us. My parents are also coming for the occasion and it looks like we will have two families staying and dining as guests of *Simpler Times*," Rose exclaimed energetically.

"Wow, well that sounds perfect. What can I help with?" Maggie inquired.

"I'm going to jot down my menu this evening and perhaps you could stop over tomorrow for lunch and we can discuss how to set the tables and if you would like to bring a dish or two. It certainly isn't necessary, but I wouldn't say no either," Rose laughed.

"Ok, I can do that. I will come over about noon tomorrow if that works."

"Yes, that's great. The girls will have just had lunch and be down for a nap. So, I'll see you then."

"Great. Bye, Rose." Maggie replied and pushed the 'end call' button on her phone. Still feeling energetic and generally content, Maggie grabbed her scissors from under the counter and started breaking open the large brown boxes of fun that had been calling her name since yesterday.

CHAPTER 12

Rose sat at her little kitchen table jotting down notes on a tablet she pulled from her junk drawer.

-Menu:
-Turkey
-Stuffing
-Mashed potatoes and gravy
-Corn soufflé
-Roasted buttercup squash
-Dinner rolls

*Delegate who is bringing sides and desserts. Have to have pumpkin pie and cranberries for sure. Wine is a must.

In the middle of jotting down her notes of when to invite guests over, Rose lifted her pen and stared out the small window in her kitchen. She was picturing Cherish. Her inn. The new bite of cool air. Her thoughts drifted back to the Thanksgiving Day she had spent (or so she thought) entertaining and so truly enjoying her friends there. Her heart almost ached when she remembered Mudsie coming early that morning to help her with the dinner prep work. Like Rose's mom had advised, Mudsie told her to have a glass of wine prior to her guest's arrival. One glass. It only made sense. Nurse the glass of Chardonnay while you're basting the turkey, mashing the spuds, pulling apart steaming hot dinner rolls. You will end up being a perfect host by the last sip.

Mudsie was so real. Rose remembered her tissue paper thin skin, age marked and soft as satin, rubbing her hand when she was anxious or missing her Flynn. Mudsie had smile creases, not frown creases, despite the unlucky cards life had dealt her. She was real. She lived. Damn it, Rose knew it. Somehow, she knew her dear, sweet old friend could not be a figment of her imagination. It was too much to bear.

Wiping a surprising tear from her cheek, Rose came back to reality. Standing, she grabbed her mug and walked to the coffee maker for a refill. In memory of Mudsie, or in honor rather, Rose agreed coffee could always make one feel better.

A knock at the front door interrupted Rose as she poured the heavy cream into her coffee causing a swirl of black and white.

Rose walked to the front door, opening it for her guest.

"Maggie, come in! I was just starting to write a few notes about Thanksgiving. Let's go to the kitchen," Rose exclaimed. Maggie smiled. She hung her wool coat on the coat tree and followed Rose into the kitchen.

"Mmmmm, Rose do you ever not have something wonderful smelling up your kitchen?" Maggie asked, inhaling deeply.

Rose smiled. "I can't have people over without serving something tasty. You've known me for a little while, Maggie. Is it not true?"

"Well, yes, I guess that is true. I have yet to come over when there is not a bundt cake, a loaf of bread or a prime rib in the oven," Maggie replied honestly.

"It's my joy, Maggie. Just accept it. That's what I told my husband," Rose winked. "And today I made chicken and broccoli tetrazzini for lunch. Please tell me you haven't eaten yet."

The two friends sat and enjoyed a helping of the pasta dish Rose had prepared along with a small caprese salad bursting with color and pungent flavor. Dabbing the corners of her mouth with the cloth napkin she held on her lap, Rose finally spoke. "So, Maggie. I am planning to have guests arrive for Thanksgiving dinner at 1:00 p.m. I was wondering if you wanted to come a bit early and share a glass of wine while I complete the last bits of prep work."

Maggie laughed, "Well certainly I would love to, but I most definitely will not just be watching you work. I will help wherever needed. My mother is elderly now, but I'm sure she would enjoy sitting next to the fire with a warm cup of cider or a glass of wine herself. I want to help you out. I know the work that goes into these things."

Rose exhaled dramatically, "Excellent. I was hoping you would say that. But I hated to come right out and ask!"

CHAPTER 13

Maggie spent the rest of the afternoon doing some much needed housework she had been avoiding. The shop had been keeping her busy, her newfound friendship with Rose had been occupying a lot of her time too, though she wasn't unhappy about it. Plus, who really wants to wipe down kitchen cabinets, dust ceiling fans and reorganize the entryway closet anyway? But, it needed to be done, among other household duties. Maggie always found it bearable with a little background music, so she turned her radio on to the oldies station–103.5 FM. As she squeezed the soapy water from her rag and began wiping down her cream colored cabinets, the radio played favorite tunes from years past. Maggie hummed to *Wouldn't it be Nice* by the Beach Boys and even did a little dance across the kitchen floor while Billy Joel's voice filled the room with his hit *Uptown Girl*. After scrubbing and dusting, Maggie took a quick bathroom break before she dug into the closet. She was feeling so light on her feet today, things were going well in her life and she was grateful for it. After washing her hands and running a brush through her hair and tying it back again, she was ready to dig into more projects downstairs. Skipping down the staircase, she stopped dead in her tracks on the last step. Her heart sped up and her hand on the banister began to perspire. She could hear the words being sung so sweetly from the kitchen- *They asked me how I knew my true love was true, Oh oh oh oh, I, of course, replied, something here inside cannot be denied...* It was strange really, that for a year of listening to oldies as Maggie did, she hadn't heard their song, her and Samuel's song, in the entire time since he had died. *Smoke Gets in Your Eyes* by the Platters. It was their wedding song and their slow dancing melody on late nights in the kitchen while they sipped wine. Samuel would try to sing along and serenade Maggie, though it mostly brought her giggles, which he equally loved.

Maggie stood for a minute longer holding on to the banister before she walked into the kitchen. Walking past her sparkling clean cabinets, she went to look out at the pond where the swan couple always returned. In this cold, gray November, the pond was without their presence again. Gripping the windowsill with her fingers, she listened to the final lyrics of the song, *Now, laughing friends deride tears I cannot hide, Oh oh oh oh oh, so I smile and say, when a lovely flame dies, smoke gets in your eyes.*

The lump in her throat turned into a sob. Maggie slid to the floor and cried until she was exhausted. When her eyes were feeling dry and itchy she stood up and grabbed a napkin from the counter and blew her nose. At this point, three or four songs had played to the lonely room and Maggie was past ready for bed. She turned the radio off and flicked off the lights and slowly walked back up the stairs to her bedroom.

Tomorrow was another day.

CHAPTER 14

"Come in, come in, Maggie! Mom and I are just starting to get things prepared for dinner." Rose exclaimed excitedly as she welcomed Maggie through the front door.

"Thank you, Rose. Before I walk into the kitchen and embarrass myself, can you tell me your mother's name again?" Maggie whispered.

Rose laughed.

"Evie. And my dad is Philip. He's outside gathering firewood with Flynn. We have to have a crackling fire in the fireplace today. First one this fall. Mmmmm. The temps dropped a bit last night, there's a cool chill in the air and a damp scent that reminds me of the season that is coming soon." Rose inhaled deeply.

"You should be a writer, Rose. So, descriptive." Maggie commented with a smile.

The two friends shared a quick embrace and Maggie remembered the bag of goodies for the Thanksgiving meal.

"I almost forgot. I made a Dutch apple pie. And decided to bring a quart of my mom's pickled beets, a bottle of my favorite wine and a lovely smelling candle from my shop for the host!"

Maggie handed the pie and the bag of items to Rose, as they walked toward the kitchen.

"You're so kind, Maggie. Thank you. Why did your mother decide not to come along? I was anxious to meet her." Rose pushed open the swinging door that led into her kitchen.

"Ohhh, she was excited too, but a couple of days ago she came down with a little sniffle and she didn't want to travel. Her neighbor insisted she join them for dinner though, and that is only walking distance. I am going to drive up there and visit her on Sunday," Maggie explained.

The tantalizing smells of buttery dinner rolls baking, juicy turkey slices stacked warm on an oval platter and the slight herby scent of rosemary and sage filled the room. A woman about ten to fifteen years older than Maggie sat on a wooden stool at the counter scooping bright orange flesh from a steaming buttercup squash into a white porcelain serving bowl. When she heard the women enter the kitchen, she turned around and smiled. Maggie could see the resemblance. Both Evie and Rose had the same round shaped blue eyes, fair skin and though Evie kept her hair shoulder length, Maggie could tell that it had once been the same full, wavy hair that Rose kept so beautifully cared for.

Evie jumped off her stool and eagerly walked over to Maggie.

"You must be Maggie? I'm so happy to finally meet you! Rose and Flynn have only wonderful things to say about you."

Maggie blushed. "Thank you, Evie. Likewise."

"Well I should hope so from my own daughter," Evie replied, winking at Rose.

"Very funny, Mom!" Rose remarked sarcastically. "Now, let's get back down to business," she continued while she set the Dutch apple pie Maggie had brought, on to the counter.

The morning prep work proceeded, with comfortable conversation between Maggie, Rose and Evie. At one point while Rose was tending to the babies and Evie and Maggie were setting the China on the table, Flynn and Rose's father Philip walked into the living room with a large stack of firewood, freshly split. Maggie found Philip to be equally as pleasant as Evie. She continued laying forks, knives and spoons in team like fashion along with Evie laying dinner plates. The Thanksgiving meal was to be served within the hour. As Philip stoked the fire in the beautiful brick fireplace, Evie returned to the kitchen. Maggie followed hoping to help with the remaining prep work. For a time, she noticed Rose and Flynn hadn't been around.

"I wonder what is taking Rose so long upstairs. Her invited guests are set to arrive shortly," Evie said out loud.

Maggie wasn't sure if Evie had been speaking the words to her or just letting her thoughts become vocal. Either way, she had been wondering the same thing.

After what had seemed like a very long time, Rose and Flynn came down the steps, both with a sweet and cutely dressed baby in their arms.

"So sorry to leave you two in charge here. Flynn and I were talking about something important while we dressed the girls in their tights and matching dresses." Rose looked a little extra stressed than earlier, Maggie thought. She wondered why.

After Rose handed Flynn both baby girls to bring out to the living room where their toys and Jumparoos sat, she got the courage to speak.

"I don't know if this is an uncomfortable situation, Maggie, but Flynn just informed me that two of his fellow soldiers from his last deployment are going to be joining us for Thanksgiving dinner today. I'm sorry, I wasn't aware and I'm a little surprised and a smidge perturbed that Flynn would spring this on me the day of. But, evidently they didn't have anywhere else to go and he would never hear of them not having loved ones to spend this holiday with." Rose looked to her mom, Evie, who smiled softly and glanced at Maggie.

"Oh gosh, by all means. Samuel would have been the absolute same. These men are brothers, Rose. They are like blood. Not true blood, but... almost the same. Does it bring up tough memories for me–of course. But does it also bring up the nostalgia of that close knit bond Samuel had with his brothers-in-arms? It sure does. Please, don't waste another thought about it." Maggie responded truthfully, although her clammy hands were clenching the edges of her skirt.

Rose's eyes searched Maggie's for a deeper response, but smiled just the same.

"I told Flynn you would be ok with it. Thank you Maggie." Rose took a deep breath. "Ok, Mama, where are we at with the mashed potatoes?"

Before dinner, Maggie went upstairs to the bathroom to freshen up and collect herself. After leaning over the small pedestal sink and dabbing cold water on her forehead, she studied her reflection in the oval mirror. Her rich mahogany colored hair shined as it always had, her skin she had been lucky enough to keep smooth and mostly without wrinkles just yet, but her eyes couldn't lie. Could eyes ever not show the truth, Maggie thought? Fright, Joy, Humiliation, Sadness… The eyes were a giveaway. Why now was Maggie having a moment? Was it the nostalgia of the holiday and family closeness here in Rose's home? Or was it the mention of military friends coming to join the group for dinner? Perhaps a combination. But, either way, Maggie stared back at herself in the mirror and took a deep breath and then another. She closed her eyes and saw a glimpse of her favorite daydream behind those closed lids, smiling back at her. Samuel's smooth, freshly shaved cheeks made her yearn to run her fingertips across them, his grin causing hers to come back to life. His eyes, so crystal light blue, they stared through her. And they did. They always did. He could read her like an open book. Could sense her despair, her elation, her every stress and emotion.

"Samuel, help." Maggie whispered to the quiet bathroom, with her eyes still shut. For what seemed like several moments, she felt a sudden calmness and could almost hear Samuel's voice saying two simple words—"Find Faith."

Maggie's lip trembled. "I'm trying, Samuel. But it isn't so easy letting you go."

Realizing now was not the time to have a breakdown, Maggie decided on the opposite. Straightening her hair in the mirror and inhaling a deep, cleansing breath of air, she reached for the door and headed for the stairway.

CHAPTER 15

"**O**h, goodness, there you are Maggie. I was worried you had gotten sick or something," Rose exclaimed as she came through the swinging kitchen door, grabbing Maggie's hand.

"I'm sorry. Was I up there long?" Maggie apologized.

"It seemed like it. Mom even asked if I should go check on you."

Rose noticed she was making Maggie feel embarrassed. and shaking her head, she brushed it off and changed the subject.

"Let's go put the finishing touches on dinner. Most of our guests have already arrived and have refreshments by the warm fire Flynn and Dad started."

Maggie followed Rose back to the kitchen. As far as she could tell, dinner looked ready to serve.

"What can I do?" Maggie asked. She noticed Evie was ladling the gravy into a large antique gravy boat and with the edge of her apron wiped the few drips from the edge. Things had to be perfectly presentable.

"Here Maggie, would you bring out these two bottles of wine and offer a refill, while Mom and I get the last items set out on the table?" Rose asked while handing Maggie a bottle of Chardonnay and Pinot Noir.

"Yes, of course."

Maggie carried the bottles of wine into the sitting room where several guests were mingling, visiting and warming themselves by the fire. She noticed Clem, Nora and Nora's husband, Chad, laughing together in the corner of the room. Nearby in two arm chairs were Mr. and Mrs. Pumpernickel sipping glasses of a deep red liquid, which Maggie knew would be the Pinot Noir she held in her left hand. Rose's dad, Philip was in the back of the room making cute faces at his granddaughters as they bounced in their little bouncy chairs. Flynn stoked the fire while two young men stood military straight next to him deep in conversation. Maggie swallowed hard, realizing those men obviously were Flynn's Army friends. Maggie stood still, a little nervous, wondering where to start, when someone interrupted her sudden trance.

"Maggie, hello. I didn't know you would be here today. Nice surprise."

Maggie turned toward the voice to see Stuart Vontrapp standing next to her.

"Oh, Stuart. Hi. I, well, I guess I didn't know who was on the list either, to be honest."

Looking down at her hands, Stuart commented, "Can I be of assistance? I can pour the red if you want to pour the white?"

Maggie smiled, "That sounds good to me. Thank you Stuart."

After the two made a pass through the room, topping off several glasses, Rose made the announcement that dinner was ready and wanted to offer a prayer beforehand. All in attendance bowed their heads and listened to Rose give thanks for the dinner and the friends and family there to enjoy it together.

Rose then led the way to the dining room where the table was set beautifully. Maggie waited until the last folks filed into the dining room and then followed. Not surprising, the room almost glowed with Autumn warmth. The table was set with antique China etched in gold, brown and burgundy leaves. White cloth napkins were folded next to place cards scrolled with each guest's name. The centerpiece Maggie loved, but would have never thought of herself. Three very large, white pillar candles were lit and surrounded by deer antlers, small oak twigs and acorns that Maggie could only assume came from the very back yard behind Rose's house. Maggie loved it and took note of future ideas for the store.

"Maggie, it looks like you are sitting by me." Clem called when he saw her walking into the room.

She was glad someone noticed and could give her direction. Today, she was a bit off, and happy for any guidance she was given.

The large oval table seated twelve, but there were two additional tables set up in the room that each seated six. Maggie noticed many she didn't recognize, people staying at the Inn she guessed. But at the main table where she was seated next to Clem, she realized she knew most of these guests. Becoming uncomfortably aware of Stuart Vontrapp sitting right next to Caroline, his longtime admirer, Maggie felt a quick tingle in her fingertips. Why would Rose seat them together? She should know that Stuart has no feelings for Caroline. And then shocked, Maggie wondered why she cared. The moment was fleeting, but not without notice and discomfort and an unfamiliar feeling of jealousy.

After everyone was seated, napkins on laps, plates filled with juicy turkey, gravy, bright orange squash and all the fixings, Flynn stood up with his glass of wine and offered a toast.

"Rose and I are so excited to have you all here to enjoy our first Thanksgiving dinner at *Simpler Times*. This has been a dream come true, more than you know." Flynn looked down at his young wife and winked.

"We hope it will be the first of many. And please know each and every one of you are always welcome." Flynn raised his glass.

"A toast to our family, friends, *Simpler Times* and our new life here in Crosby."

Flynn leaned down and kissed Rose while everyone smiled and clinked their glasses together.

Maggie and Clem raised their glasses to cheers, but Maggie glanced a second time at Stuart and Caroline across the table. Why hadn't she noticed that Stuart was handsome before. At least, she was seeing something in that category that apparently the townspeople didn't. Well, all except Caroline who was sitting next to him, and relishing every minute.

Maggie sliced bits of her turkey, took small bites of her mashed potatoes and gravy while Clem carried on about the price of gas going up. To Maggie it started to sound like the adult voices on episodes of Charlie Brown.

What the heck is wrong with me? Maggie asked herself internally.

Finally, relieved that guests started excusing themselves from the table for a stroll in the yard or a sit on the front porch, Maggie did the same and retreated to the kitchen where she would offer her help to wash dishes.

CHAPTER 16

Rose had given Marie and Lucille Thanksgiving Day off to be with family, but they had returned to work the morning after to clean rooms and take over breakfast duties for Rose. Rose and Flynn took advantage of the rare moment together and bundled up Jade and Sophia for a walk down Main Street, Crosby. Now that Thanksgiving had been celebrated and the holiday season had officially kicked off, the town was a bustle. Especially given the unseasonably mild temps for late November in Minnesota, the couple couldn't pass up a stroll with the girls.

"Sophia, let me tie your bonnet. It's chilly." Rose begged, while the rosy cheeked baby fussed and tugged at the satin ribbon under her chin.

"Ahh, Rosebud, just leave it untied. She's snug in her stroller seat with a fuzzy blanket. They'll probably sweat even." Flynn teased.

" Well, I guess. But my mom always told me to bundle babies up, nice and cozy warm. It rings in my head and I maybe get too carried away."

"It's sweet, Rose. You're a doting mom who is trying her very best. Out of the one million and two things I love about you, seeing you as a mother to our girls is at the top of the list," Flynn told her honestly and tucked her mitten covered hand around his arm.

Flynn pushed the double stroller up the sidewalk while Rose admired the town's people busily decorating store fronts and street lamps. The city workers were high up on ladders hanging large green wreaths complete with burgundy colored bows attached. Rose noticed twinkling white lights in the window of *Cream and Sugar* and got a sudden urge for a warm drink in her hand.

"Flynn, let's grab a coffee for the walk. Here, let's cross right here."

Flynn opened the large glass door of *Cream and Sugar* for his wife and pushed the stroller through. The coffee shop was busy, but the line wasn't too long. The regulars sat at corner tables, while visitors sat up at the window counter busy on their laptops or watching the action outside while they finished their cinnamon scones and cheese bagels.

"Well, hi you two," Nora greeted, as Rose and Flynn made their way up to the front of the line to place their order. "Thank you again for such a wonderful dinner yesterday. Chad and I didn't think we would ever be hungry again, but somehow found our way to those pieces of apple pie you sent home with us—oh, about nine o'clock last night."

Rose and Flynn laughed.

"I'm so glad you could make it Nora. It was a wonderful day," Rose agreed.

Flynn looked at the chalkboard menu on the wall, deciding on what he was in the mood for.

"Nora, I'm going to be adventurous and have an Americana, black." Flynn said, winking.

"Ahhh, adventurous you say huh?" Nora laughed. "And you Rose?"

"I'll have a latte with oat milk and lavender foam. Something different. I'm usually on team Americana like Flynn, but what the heck—it's a festive day."

Nora nodded and said, "Coming right up. And it's on the house today. You did enough yesterday. A coffee on me is the least I can do."

"Thanks Nora. But, that's not necessary." Flynn replied, throwing a twenty dollar bill in the tip jar. "But, if you insist, then we will be generous to the tip fund."

"Fine. That's fair. And thank you."

Nora slid two foam cups into cardboard sleeves and handed them to Rose and Flynn.

"Have a nice stroll through town. See you soon," she called as the couple waved and left.

"Ok, Rosebud, which way?" Flynn asked.

"Well, let's make our way down to Maggie's shop, cross the street and head down to the park. They are having carolers, a tree lighting and other fun activities there too." Rose answered, excitedly. She had always loved holidays, especially the Christmas season. She became like a little kid, giddy with anticipation and joy.

Flynn and Rose walked and sipped their beverages in silence for a couple of blocks while they kept admiring their quaint small town. Rose felt like they were both thinking the same thing, without speaking the words out loud. *How lucky we are to have found this town and have the opportunity to make Simpler Times a reality. Especially after all we have been through.* Life dealt some unsure cards, but once in a while, with luck (and a steadfast trust in God's plan) you ended up with a royal flush. That was how Flynn and Rose felt—so very lucky.

"Awwww, look at Maggie's shop!" Rose commented admiringly, as they neared *The Maple Leaf.* The two large showcase windows on either side of the entrance were etched with fake snow, the kind you sprayed lightly to look like frost. It looked so real and sparkled just like when you would wake up and look out the window to a fresh, crystal snowfall on tree branches. Large bunches of evergreen garland hung above the windows and across the window boxes in front. Maggie had set large, vintage sleigh bells in the window boxes atop the evergreen branches. On the sidewalk just before entering the store sat a large black lantern with a white pillar candle flickering inside. Rose assumed the candle was fake, but it certainly looked real.

"Rosebud, should we go in and say hi or are you going to just sit out here admiring the decorations?" Flynn teased.

"Oh, right," Rose giggled and lightly punched Flynn's arm.

Not surprisingly, the inside of Maggie's shop was transforming into what looked like a lovely Christmas movie scene. Maggie's classic, vintage style reminded Rose of one of her favorites during the holidays—*Little Women* starring Susan Sarandon and Winona Ryder. She and Evie would watch it every year and yes, cry every year. Philip would come in the room and comment, "Why do you girls always do this to yourselves? Crying isn't fun is it? Let's watch *Die Hard* instead." Rose smiled at the brief memory.

Maggie's head popped out from behind a large armoire set up in the center of the room, when she heard the front doorbells jingle.

"Can I help y–, Oh, well this is a pleasant surprise. Even Flynn and the babies are here to visit!" Maggie exclaimed.

"Yes, Lucille and Marie demanded they take over entirely with breakfast and cleaning this morning and sent us out for a leisurely walk," Rose answered.

"How nice! Let me look at Jade and Sophia. Are they enjoying it too?"

"Well, they usually conk out when we take them out in the stroller," Flynn said as he pulled back the blanket. "Yep, look at that."

Both Jade and Sophia lay deep in sleep while the three adults sighed.

"Awwww, what little peanuts. They look so angelic sleeping in those matching white bonnets, Rose. Where did you find them fringed with puffy white fur? Too cute!" Maggie complimented.

"My mom. I don't know where she finds these things. But, they are cute aren't they? You need to see the little ruffled tights she sent for them too!"

"Ok, this is where I walk next door to the *Pumpernickel House* to sample whatever sweet rolls Mabel is pulling from the oven," Flynn sighed, in mock annoyance. "I'll be back in a bit, Rose."

"Men!" Maggie snickered. "Come have a seat over here Rose. I'm just finishing this display of new holiday towels and placemats in this beautiful distressed armoire. Don't you love it? I may keep this piece for myself."

Rose pushed the stroller up next to a wingback chair and sat down. She continued sipping on her latte while Maggie pulled new green and gold hand towels from a large open box by her feet. She carefully set them in neat stacks on the shelves within the armoire and hung a few over the side of open drawers to give shoppers a better look at the design.

"I had such a wonderful time yesterday, Rose. The company was great and the food, excellent!"

"Well, thank you for helping out! It did all come together nicely, I think. Sorry, if Clem was talking your ear off during dinner. It's always challenging knowing how to set up the seating chart. Especially, since I'm just getting to know many of the people here," Rose replied as she took another peek at her daughters.

"Oh, yes. I've known Clem for years. I was happy to sit next to him. Of course, sometimes my eyes glaze over as he talks circles around the same subject without a breath in between, but that's Clem." Maggie laughed and pulled the tape off another box. "I started to wonder how he finished his plate of food, because it seemed he was only talking the entire meal."

Rose smiled. "Well, everyone seemed to get along pretty well. Stuart and Caroline were laughing together, Mr. and Mrs. Pumpernickel seemed so relaxed and comfortable. Even our many guests at the Inn, new to our Thanksgiving table, were, seemingly, having a good time."

"Yes. It was a perfect day," Maggie responded and turned back to her task of unloading the box of hand woven placemats. "I was a little surprised you had sat Stuart next to Caroline, though. But, I know you said it's challenging to know where to put everyone, so I completely understand."

Rose thought she noticed Maggie to be slightly flustered, and wondered why. The comment about Stuart and Caroline, was also a bit of a mystery.

"I thought that Stuart and Caroline were friends, if not *an item*, as my grandmother would say," Rose replied.

Maggie shot a quick glance at Rose. "Ha, Stuart and Caroline? Oh my, she's been chasing him around the streets of Crosby for God knows how long, Rose. She's beautiful and all, but it's common knowledge that Stuart isn't interested. Which is why I was surprised that you sat them together at dinner yesterday."

Rose started to wonder, but shook her head and thought, *No, Maggie couldn't, could she?*

"Maggie, you don't have an—" Rose started to ask a question and was cut off by the front door bells.

Flynn walked in with a half-eaten apple fritter in his hand and a large bite still being chewed in his puffed out cheek. Finally swallowing he spoke, "Ready Rosebud? If you want to hit the park festivities, we better get gettin!"

"Yes, of course. Let's get going. Maggie, do you want to join us?"

"Oh, no thank you. I have lots to do here today. You go check it out and have a good time!" Maggie answered, waving them off.

Rose studied her friend for a moment. "Ok, Mags. I will check in with you soon. Have fun doing your thing today. The shop already looks magical."

Flynn and Rose walked out to the sidewalk again and began down the direction of the park.

Rose couldn't stop thinking about Maggie's strange behavior minutes ago. It almost seemed like she was jealous of Caroline getting close to Stuart. *No, I was imagining things. I'm sure of it. Maggie has never seemed even remotely interested in dating and has never given a second thought to Stuart Vontrapp. Or had things changed somehow?*

"Rose. Rose? We just walked past one of the families staying at *Simpler Times* and you didn't even say hello. Are you daydreaming?" Flynn questioned.

"What? Oh, no, did I? Sorry. I don't know, I guess I was pondering some comments Maggie had made back at her store while you had been at *Pumpernickel House.*"

"Oh, is she ok? Did having my Army buddies present at dinner yesterday stir up fresh memories of Samuel? I was hoping that wouldn't happen. Shoot," Flynn complained as his mouth tilted into a concerned grimace.

"No, no. It wasn't that. But, you're right, I too had a tiny worry about that detail. She was, and maybe I was imagining it, but it almost seemed as if she had a spark of jealousy over Stuart and Caroline."

"What? Well, that would be the best thing for her. Not the jealousy part, but just that she is finally ready, even slightly ready, to date again? That is a good thing. It's been over a year of solid heartache. I didn't know Samuel, but had I been in his shoes, I would have wanted you to move on, Rosebud." Flynn responded.

"Yes, I would have to agree. Well, I'm not going to pry just yet. Maybe things will naturally play out. If there is something there—it won't stay hidden forever."

Flynn and Rose entered the gates to the large town park just as a massive pine was being lit with colorful Christmas lights and the high school choir began the first verse of *Oh Come All Ye Faithful.*

CHAPTER 17

December 1st was when the first snowfall hit Crosby. Maggie started her Jeep from inside the house with her remote starter on her keychain. *What a genius invention,* she thought. Though it was cold and wet and she would most likely have to shovel the sidewalk in front of the store entrance by day's end, she had to admit it was beautiful. Still dark outside at this early hour, she could only see the glisten of the snowflakes fall near the glow from the light post in her front yard. Luckily, she had already set up small evergreen trees in various sizes under the light post. She loved the look of snow lightly covering the pine needles of each branch and the shine above making it glisten. That was another one of her mother's ideas, and she loved it.

Taking one last bite of her sourdough toast followed by a sip of milk, she set her dishes in the sink and headed for the closet in search of snow boots, a hat and a pair of warm mittens. Maggie wondered if the snowfall would bring more customers or hinder folks from venturing out on the potentially slick roads. Christmas cheer was in the air and what better to get people in the mood to shop than the first snow of the year. But again, she never could guess. It was supposed to keep on all day, and roads may get sketchy. Either way, she zipped up her coat, grabbed her purse and closed the door behind her, eager to open the shop at 9:00 a.m. sharp.

Despite the increasingly heavy snowfall, Main Street was busy as ever. School evidently was still running on time as a few school buses were stopped here and there at intersections, picking up students bundled up for the elements. Maggie saw Clem outside his store front shoveling the first three inches of snow. *Cream and Sugar* was just as busy as any usual morning. Business owners apparently still needed a *pick me up* no matter the weather, I guess. A puff of warm fragrant air was visible from the vents out front of the dry cleaners shop in the contrasting cool temps. The post office was lit bright, as was the corner gas station, the yoga studio and *Pumpernickel House* as she turned the corner to park in the back lot of *The Maple Leaf.* Soon, Maggie too, would join the busyness that was mornings on Main Street.

Fidgeting with her key in the lock while still donning her large mittens, Maggie noticed the corner of an envelope or possibly a piece of notebook paper peeking out from under the lip of the door. Given the tin box attached to the ledge out front for mail, she didn't have a clue what this could be. Finally, turning the bronze knob to the right, the door clicked and pushed open. Maggie kicked the snow from her boots and stepped in, being careful not to step on whatever mail had been delivered in an unusual fashion. Without taking the time to remove her damp mittens and coat, she leaned down and grabbed the unmarked envelope. *Strange, why not drop in the mailbox out front?* Maggie thought.

Ripping the seal open, she pulled out a note.

Maggie,

This may seem forward, but I was wondering if you would ever consider meeting for coffee or taking a walk with me? Your teeth are near perfect so we don't get the opportunity to see each other all that often. It was so enjoyable to spend some time with you on Thanksgiving Day at the Mitchells. This has been on my mind, however I haven't had the guts to talk to you in person about it. Perhaps, this mysterious note will give you the time to consider my offer as well as ponder if you are ready for such. Much respect for either answer I receive.

Sincerely,
Stuart

Maggie just about dropped the handwritten letter on the floor after reading it. She had absolutely no idea Stuart had even an inkling of feelings for her. Sure, he had come into the store for help with gift baskets here and there, but Maggie thought that was a genuine lack of knowledge in the "shopping for women" department.

Perhaps, it was a little of both.

And had she taken a keen interest in how much he and Caroline had giggled and visited across the table from her on Thanksgiving Day? She remembered feeling a little queasy when Caroline would touch Stuart's shoulder. And she certainly wasn't paying attention to what Clem was talking about. Poor Clem. How rude she must've seemed. But Maggie had noticed Stuart that day, in a way she hadn't before.

What has changed? she wondered.

Suddenly, it all seemed like an inappropriate affair. Like a movie where the good guy is betrayed. Samuel was barely gone from this earth and she was having little thoughts about another man? Jealousy had even consumed her briefly on, of all days, Thanksgiving Day. No, she wasn't ready for this. She shouldn't be. It wasn't right. For now, she would pretend the letter never made it into her hands. She would act cordial, but generic, if she ran into Stuart. That was the right thing to do and the way she wanted things to remain.

Maggie crumpled up the letter and the envelope it was delivered in and tossed it in the trash can. After doing so, she hung her wet coat, mittens and hat on the hooks next to the door and slid her boots off, setting them on the boot tray next to a heater.

"Kitty, kitty?" She called for her fluffy cat. She had made the decision a month or so ago to adopt a sweet pet to live at *The Maple Leaf.* It had been fun having a little friend to keep her company on the slow rainy days when she would rearrange the cabinets and mark down prices on items that were out of season.

"Kitty? Muffin? Where are you? Always hiding from me aren't you?" She teased, looking under tables and behind bookshelves.

"Aha! I should have known. Your favorite cozy hideaway."

Maggie found the gray and white fuzzy cat curled up in a ball between an oversized throw pillow propped against the wall and a basket filled with handmade socks and slippers.

The cat, Muffin, yawned and stretched all four legs, without a care in the world. Maggie laughed and petted her on the head between the ears.

"Awwww, Muffin- you sure have a chill life don't you?"

Maggie walked around the shop, clicking on lamps and plugging in strings of twinkly Christmas lights that she had strung here and there. As usual she turned on mood music. Today, she decided on some holiday favorites from the past. Bing Crosby's voice sang *White Christmas* through the speaker, and it sure fit the day, Maggie thought.

"Ok, what do we start with today, Muffin?"

Deciding on trimming a small artificial tree with new ornaments she had just ordered last week, Maggie grabbed a box and walked to the front of the store where a large display window sat. The original shop was beautifully built with two large curved windows where past shop owners would display items for sale. There were two steps to the large platform which sat behind the window. Samuel knew Maggie would love the classic look of this part of the shop and so they kept it as is, maintaining it as needed.

With the tree set up and colorful lights clipped on the branches, Maggie kneeled down and began hanging the ornaments she pulled from boxes. Again, being a fan of nostalgia and all things old fashioned, though these ornaments were brand new, they looked like vintage glass bulbs. They were of various colors, but had that old worn, sort of tarnished look. Maggie felt as if she had grown up in the early part of the 1900s rather than the latter. She felt the same when her and Rose visited. Rose had told her a little about an old fashioned town she had visited once that almost seemed like it had been stuck back in time. But Rose never went into great detail about the town before changing the subject. Maggie couldn't quite understand why Rose had always seemed a little sad when she mentioned that place.

"Ok, now a star for the top. Where did I put that? I had it right here, I thought." Maggie said out loud to herself. She scrounged through the boxes, pulling out tissue paper and bubble wrap, tipping both boxes upside down and ducking under the tree in case it had fallen underneath. At that moment she heard the front doorbells jingle and footsteps.

"Anybody here? Maggie? Oh, there you are? What are you doing halfway under this lovely decorated Christmas tree?" a man's voice asked.

Embarrassed, Maggie backed out from under the tree and stood up, noticing it was Stuart.

Why did it have to be him that paid her a surprise visit while she was crouched halfway under a Christmas tree, butt up in the air and pine needles stuck in her hair?

Standing up and brushing the pine needles off her shirt and dust from her pants, she managed to say hello to Stuart, pink rising into her cheeks.

"Hi, Stuart. How are you? Managing the blizzard ok?" Maggie decided to act generically as she had promised herself to do earlier, though she didn't think she would run into Stuart so soon after the note he had left.

"Well, yes, so far so good. That's kind of what I stopped in about. I wanted you to know I shoveled out front here and had some extra salt that I sprinkled on the sidewalk for you. Don't want Mabel slipping when she runs over a few of her freshly baked Spritz cookies."

"Oh, I totally forgot about doing that. My gosh, thank you Stuart. You didn't have to do that!" Maggie fidgeted.

"Not a problem at all. I had my boots and snow stuff on after shoveling in front of the dental office and so I thought, "Why not take care of *Pumpernickel House* and *The Maple Leaf* while I'm on a roll." Stuart replied, humbly.

"Well, I really appreciate it," Maggie answered.

Remembering her guilt from earlier, she began stuffing tissue paper back into the cardboard boxes and busily moving about the display window.

"Oh, my Stuart, I still have a ton to do today. I better get to it." She glanced out the window to her freshly shoveled sidewalk. "And thank you again for doing that. The shoveling I mean. Very neighborly of you."

Stuart's face had a look of disappointment, but he quickly recovered with a white toothy grin. "You are very welcome, Maggie. Have a good day, and stay safe on the roads."

The door closed behind him and she looked up to see him walking back toward his dental office, his shovel and a small bucket of salt in either hand.

This feeling didn't sit right either!

What had Maggie gotten herself into??

CHAPTER 18

Rose whistled to the radio as an instrumental version of *Have Yourself a Merry Little Christmas* played. She was seasoning pork sausage patties she had hand formed and laid neatly on cookie sheets, with sage and poultry seasoning. Her grandma had made these often at Monday morning breakfasts years ago, and it was popular with guests staying at *Simpler Times* also. She shoved the sheets into the oven and set the timer for thirty minutes, then walked to the refrigerator. Pulling out a carton of eggs and a large bowl of blueberries, she continued her morning breakfast prep. All the while still whistling to the cheery holiday tunes playing on her small kitchen radio. Her mom tried to buy her an Echo dot so she could tell *Alexa* what song to play, but as always, Rose preferred the oldies station. She didn't want to boss a virtual lady around. This was the way she liked it.

"Rose? The table is set and coffee is perking in the dining room. Should I bring out the butter dishes and salt and pepper sets?" Lucille asked as she walked into the kitchen.

Rose wiped her hands on her apron and looked up at the wall clock.

"Yes, I think that would be just fine, Lucille. We should be ready to serve in about thirty minutes or so. Thank you."

"Of course," Lucille answered and started placing sets of salt and pepper shakers on a wooden tray.

Rose glanced at Lucille and smiled. She felt so fortunate to have her and Marie's help around the Inn. With caring for the babies and Flynn back to work and word traveling fast about *Simpler Times*, she was as busy as she could be.

Returning to her task at hand, she reached below the butcher block for a large glass mixing bowl and started cracking eggs into it, a tablespoon of vanilla extract, some milk and ground cinnamon were tossed in and she whisked it until smooth. The griddle was greased, hot and ready for slabs of french toast to be cooked on top. Rose started dredging slices of homemade french bread in the egg mixture and laid each in rows on her griddle. As they quickly sizzled, the warm, enticing scent of cinnamon filled the kitchen. No doubt both the smell of the sausage in the oven and the french toast cooking on the griddle was rising up the stairs and waking hungry guests. When all the pieces of french toast had been set in large baking pans, Rose covered them quickly with tin foil and set in the standing warmer until she was ready to serve the morning meal. After the sausage was taken from the oven, Lucille returned to the kitchen.

"I will wash the blueberries, Rose. Then all we need is powdered sugar, maple syrup and the jar of your homemade clotted cream. The buffet is ready with serving utensils and trivets set out for the hot platters," Lucille told Rose, while she worked on washing the blueberries, then pouring them into a beautiful Jadeite bowl.

"Perfect! It somehow always comes together doesn't it Lucille?" Rose replied. "Ok, sausage is done and plated. Let's bring it all out."

A few families were enjoying a cup of coffee or cocoa by the fire, while folks that enjoyed sleeping in were just coming down the staircase. As informed at check-in that breakfast was served in the dining room at 9:00 a.m. sharp, everyone made their way down the hallway to that room. After all guests were seated Rose greeted them and offered a prayer before their meal.

"Again, thank you all for staying with us here at *Simpler Times*. We are so happy to have you. Lucille and I have set up the buffet with the lovely dishes you are smelling. Please come on up and help yourself. If you need anything please let us know. We will be in and out checking on things and replenishing beverages."

With that, Rose and Lucille left the guests to their dining.

Lucille went back to the kitchen while Rose walked upstairs to check in on Jade and Sophia. She had fed them a couple of hours ago when they woke up. After she had changed them, Marie usually came in and watched them while Rose and Lucille made breakfast. She would lay them on a large quilt on the floor so they could kick their chubby little legs and play a bit.

Peeking her head through the doorway of the nursery, Rose softly spoke, "How are we doing in here? Marie, have my babies been good girls for you?"

Marie was sitting on the quilt next to the girls holding a story book in her hands. She was about sixty years old or so, Rose guessed, and thought it was important to read to children from the day they were born. Jade and Sophia were so used to it that they seemed more content and joyful when the comforting sound of Marie's voice was reading the words of *The Velveteen Rabbit* or *Winnie the Pooh*.

"Of course, always. These little cherubs never give me a hard time, Rose," Marie replied.

Rose laughed. "I guess they save the trying times for their mama and daddy."

She picked up a squirmy Jade while Marie scooped up little Sophia.

"Let's bring them downstairs for a bit. They love to sit in their highchairs and watch us work in the kitchen," Rose suggested. "You can start stripping beds and getting loads of sheets in the wash if you'd like Marie? The girls will be content sitting in their highchairs for some time now."

"That sounds good, Rose," she said, smiling at the girls.

Rose glanced out the second story window of her babies' bedroom and watched the soft snowflakes swirling in the air. So pure, clean and simple. It had started to accumulate a thick blanket of white on the ground that was reminiscent of fluffy clouds—like a dream.

She whispered in Jade's little pink ear, "this time it is a dream come true."

Jade's tiny fingers reached up and touched her mother's cheek.

Rose sometimes worried that the beauty of her life and the dreams that had become a reality would be snatched away again, like they had been before. But, she knew in her heart that things had turned out how they were meant to.

Still, she never took any of the blessings in her life for granted. And the simple sight of snowfall and a soft baby hand touching her cheek were no exception.

CHAPTER 19

"So, Maggie—I want you to give me some holiday centerpiece ideas for my dining room table. Guests keep *Simpler Times'* rooms filled and I know it won't slow down this month. I realized that I need to spruce things up a bit. No pun intended," Rose winked.

"Oh gosh, you don't need me, Rose. Your Thanksgiving table was absolutely beautiful. Simple and lovely. Something I would never have even thought of, but it worked," Maggie answered back.

"Well, I appreciate that. But Maggie, I sometimes run out of creativity, what with planning diverse meals, decorating the Inn and adding some memorable touches—my palette goes dry," Rose responded with a sigh.

"How poetic, Rose," Maggie laughed. She jumped off her stool. "Ok, let's walk around the store and see what hits us, shall we?"

As Rose grabbed jar candles off a shelf and smelled each, she decided she'd casually bring up something about Stuart Vontrapp and see if it hit a nerve with Maggie.

After smelling the black licorice candle and grimacing, Rose cleared her throat and just came out with it.

"So, have you helped Stuart Vontrapp with any more gift shopping? I'm sure he will be needing assistance with Christmas presents."

Maggie stopped studying her table settings and looked in Rose's direction.

"Why would I have any idea about that? I don't think he buys all of his gifts at my shop. And, he probably has Caroline to assist him. Though, she probably only shops at designer stores in the metro."

There it was *again*, Rose noticed. It was unmistakable this time. Maggie was jealous of Caroline getting close to Stuart, which could only mean one thing.... She had feelings for Stuart. On some level at least, she had to. Rose decided to tread lightly with this conversation.

"Oh, I like this table, Maggie," she said pointing at a large, rectangle table. It was set with wooden chargers and red and green plaid dinner plates on top. Clear stemmed water glasses were paired to each place setting. A very large hurricane vase sat in the center of the table filled with cranberries and a singular white pillar candle. The colors popped, but the simplicity remained intact. *Perfect,* Rose thought, almost becoming completely distracted from their discussion a few minutes ago.

"I love this, actually. Do you have these items in stock or would you have to order, Maggie?" Rose asked, while studying one of the plaid plates in her hands. "Maggie?"

Rose looked up. Maggie was looking out the shop window at something. Rose quietly walked closer behind Maggie. Surprised, but not surprised, she saw that Maggie was watching none other than Stuart walking out of *Cream and Sugar* with a brown paper bag and a drink carrier full of coffees. Every Friday he treated his employees. Community folks knew he was a wonderful person to work for and his employees agreed wholeheartedly.

Clearing her throat a second time, Rose piped up, "I like this blow up purple giraffe wearing a Santa hat. Do you think that would be pretty for a centerpiece, Mags?"

Maggie finally noticed she wasn't paying attention to Rose and stuttered.

"Yes, the giraffe, that is a great... wait, what? No, Rose. What are you saying? I don't have anything tacky like that here. What are you talking about?"

Rose walked up close to her dear friend and looked her straight in the eyes. She felt compassion for Maggie. She could see Maggie felt guilt for moving on. She had feelings for Stuart, but was interpreting them as cruel, disloyal, even dirty. Rose reached up and tucked Maggie's rich brown hair behind her ear.

"Maggie, come sit down for a minute. Let's take a break from my centerpiece obsession."

She stole one last glance out the window at Stuart greeting a couple outside his dental office, then Maggie obliged.

"I know what you're thinking, Rose. I have a thing for Stuart Vontrapp. Is that right?" Maggie questioned.

Rose crossed her legs and leaned back in the velvet arm chair she sat in, not taking her eyes off Maggie's.

"Well, if we are friends, and we are being honest, it is clear that you do, Maggie. Why are you fighting it so very hard?"

"Friends? You think you know everything about me?"

Maggie's voice became hoarse and shaky.

"Caroline annoys everyone in town, does she not? And Stuart is a decent, handsome, kind man who I just feel deserves more substance in a woman. If I have any feelings for him, it's just pity that he may have to settle for a supermodel type woman, completely void of any deep thoughts, compassion, direction."

Maggie began to obsessively rearrange a bookshelf stocked full of pouches of cookie and bread mixes. Rose watched her, but chose to not respond, just yet, to her outburst.

A pouch of gingersnap cookie mix tipped off the shelf and fell to the floor, to which Maggie's exasperated eyes followed.

"Damn it," Maggie yelled and picked up the cookie mix. She placed it back on the shelf, but not without noticing she had been behaving completely out of character. Neither her or Rose had to take any more time to guess why.

Finally Rose thought it was time to be frank with her friend.

"Maggie, it's ok. You are not betraying Samuel. It is completely natural and extremely healthy that you are starting to develop these feelings again. It has been over a year. I know this is hard. I mean, I can imagine it is hard. I thought of it countless times when Flynn was overseas. But, Flynn would have, and Samuel would now, want you to move on. And I think that he would very much approve of someone like Stuart."

Rose walked closer to Maggie, but didn't say anything more. After several moments of silence, Maggie finally turned around and looked at Rose, one tiny teardrop trickling down her left cheek.

"What am I going to do, Rose? Will you help me figure this out?"

The two friends hugged and arm and arm continued walking around *The Maple Leaf* admiring the holiday decorations Maggie had so carefully set up.

CHAPTER 20

Maggie was piling hot, cheesy eggs on top of two halves of his bagel, when she heard the shuffle of Samuel slippers behind her. When she felt his strong arms wrap around her waist, the smile couldn't be wiped from her face. She leaned her head back into the bend of his neck and he kissed her forehead.

"What's for breakfast today, Maggie? My favorite?" Samuel asked as he watched her set a few strips of bacon next to his overloaded bagels and finish with a slice of pear.

"Well, it IS your birthday. Things have to be just right. All your favorites today, my love," Maggie replied.

"You sure spoil me."

"As do you, to me. Am I wrong?" Maggie said with a wink.

"I concur," Samuel answered and took his plate to their little breakfast nook overlooking the serene pond out the front window.

As usual on spring mornings the pair of captivating swans glided down the middle of the calm glass waters. Their reflections could be seen vividly. Maggie stirred another spoonful of cream into her coffee and sat in the chair across from Samuel. She watched him enjoy his breakfast for a second before sharing in his admiration of their favorite scene outside. It had been four, maybe five years since the swans had decided to make the pond their home. They knew in April sometime, they would come back and Samuel would be looking with his binoculars every morning until they arrived. It depended much on when the Minnesota winter decided to depart. That could vary greatly. May had even been known to have a foot of snowfall. Of course, everyone knew it would melt within twenty-four hours, but just the same, snow in May? Ah, well, Samuel and Maggie would never hear of living anywhere else, snow in May or not.

"Don't you love our swans, Samuel? I hope they never leave. You know, Swans mate for life. These two have been coming here for years, and I'm certain they will continue. I mean, however long a swan's lifespan is. I guess I haven't researched that part. But either way, isn't it beautiful?" Maggie sighed while she sipped on her steaming cup of coffee.

Samuel grabbed his plate and stood up. He carried it to the sink and stood there longer than what seemed natural for the task at hand. Maggie turned and looked at him.

"What is it, Samuel? Time for work?" She asked, unnerved somehow. She watched from behind, his shoulders slumped a bit. He took one more long swallow of his coffee and set the mug in the sink too. After a couple of moments she watched as he pulled his shoulders back up and deliberately held them up straight, almost in the military march fashion she had seen him practice a time or two before. He paired the stance with what she could tell was a long, cleansing breath in. Or maybe it was a breath taken deeply in when one was hoping for courage. Maggie couldn't make sense of this moment and frankly, she didn't want to.

"Samuel, what is going on? You were just happily enjoying your birthday breakfast. Did the loyal swans' dance across the pond ruin that somehow?" Maggie asked, desperation suddenly evident in her tone.

"No. I love those swans. I've always loved the swans, Maggie. I love that even after I am no longer here, they still come to our pond. I hope that it brings you a comforting smile, rather than an ache in your heart." Samuel attempted to continue, but at his words, Maggie rose from her chair.

"You love that even after you are no longer here, they still come to our pond? Samuel, you'll have to explain. What are you talking about? You're kind of creeping me out, if I'm being honest. Why the sudden strange behavior?" Maggie wanted to run into his arms and forget this conversation, but something made her slow her pace and wait for him to continue.

Samuel turned around. He looked at Maggie with such love and hope that she could hardly feel her concern any longer.

"Maggie, I love you. I will never stop. Please know that." Samuel told her and took her left hand in his. He took another moment to find the next words.

"I want you to find faith. Finding faith in the future will keep our memory alive. Don't you see babe? Faith is all you need."

Samuel held Maggie's face in his soft hands and lightly kissed her lips. She could scarcely feel his touch. His image began to disintegrate into thin air at that moment. Strangely, Maggie wasn't scared. She was so very sad to let him go, but no longer scared. She had to find faith in her heart, have it in herself.

As the last bits of the most beautiful face she had ever seen faded like clouds in the sky before her very eyes, Maggie reached out, "Good bye Samuel. I love you."

Maggie woke to the sun shining through her window. Her cheeks were damp with tears as was the pillow where she was laying. Rolling over, she recalled her dream in almost exact detail. Closing her eyes she laid there with her hands over her face for several minutes.

"Ok, Samuel...faith. How do you *find* faith? I am trying to find it in myself. I hope that you can help me," she begged.

As Maggie had done for more days than she cared to recall since the death of her husband, she slowly pulled her patchwork quilt off and lifted one and then another leg out of bed. She forced herself to stand.

And then she started her day.

CHAPTER 21

"**F**lynn, who is going to care for the babies if we are gone for three days? And who is going to run the Inn while we are away? This doesn't sound like the best idea. Isn't it a bit irresponsible of us?" Rose said, while she washed the same dinner plate for a third time in a row.

Flynn smiled sweetly at his worrisome wife. She always had to make sure everything and everyone was taken care of. He walked over beside her and took the dinner plate from her hands.

"Rosebud, this one is very, very, clean now."

Flynn rinsed it himself and set it in the drying rack. Handing Rose a towel to dry her hands with, he continued the conversation.

"My buddy, Collins, invited us to stay a few nights at his cabin up in Manitoba, Canada. Our other friend, Sanchez, who you also met on Thanksgiving will be there too, with his wife. Rose, it is a long weekend getaway with wonderful people, I promise. I haven't made any definite plans, because I wanted to discuss things with you first. But I did run my plan by a few people that are willing to help out."

"A few people? As in?" Rose huffed, clearly agitated.

"Well, for instance—Marie and Lucille, your mom and dad. And Maggie." Flynn answered. And before Rose could question him again he added additional details within his well laid plan.

"So, your mom and dad said they will come and stay here while we are away. During the day they will work the Inn, checking guests in and out, taking money, tending to their needs and serving meals and cleaning rooms with the obvious assistance of Marie and Lucille. During the day, Maggie said she can have the girls at the shop in the back room. We would bring their Jumparoos, Pack-n-Play beds and diaper bags. In the evenings, things will be quiet at the Inn and your parents will be with Jade and Sophia for the nights."

Pacing, Rose replied, "I don't know, Flynn. This all sounds too extravagant. Leaving the Inn and leaving our daughters? And why were these buddies of yours not with their wives and families on Thanksgiving instead of here? What kind of men are they anyway?"

Rose started wiping the counter diligently with a damp wash rag as if there were deep purple beet stains that wouldn't wash off.

Flynn was sitting at the kitchen table. He reached out and pulled her onto his lap.

"Honey, it is not unusual to take a few days off. It's clear you need to learn what that means. I understand you are a new mother, but the babies will be very well cared for. As will *Simpler Times*. I have confidence in that. Please, Rosebud, you could use a little break. And maybe you will even relax and have a good time. I'd really like you to get to know Collins and Sanchez and their wives. They are the salt of the earth, Rose. Good people. After serving overseas with those two, and Marty of course, I found brothers. Bound by more than even blood." He paused, then added, "And I told you, they had training at Fort Jefferson that week, which is far from their homes and *close* to ours. So, naturally I invited them."

Rose leaned her forehead against Flynn's and sighed.

"Two things, why are Marty and Collette not attending this reunion? And why do you military guys call each other by your last names?"

Flynn laughed and kissed her cheek.

"Rosebud, Marty and Collette moved out to Massachusetts to be closer to her family, remember? They too have invited us several times, but I figured it would be a more extended trip and you most definitely aren't ready for that. And as far as the last name thing? It's just a US military thing. Everyone is known and called by their last name, and so naturally that is what we continue to refer to each other as. In fact I'm kind of unsure of Sanchez's first name even."

Rose stood up.

"Oh, oooooook! If you promise to have everything planned just perfectly, everything and everyone, most especially my sweet girls, taken care of, then I guess I will go."

"Yes! Wonderful, because I already told them we are coming."

"Flynn Mitchell!" Rose yelled in mock anger, and playfully punched his shoulder.

"Come here Rosebud." he responded, pulling her into his embrace. "You'll see, I will make sure everything and everyone is well cared for. Including this beautiful woman I'm holding."

He tipped her chin up and kissed her lips lovingly. Finally he felt her trust in him and she relaxed, returning his kiss.

CHAPTER 22

Maggie felt like a walk before starting her day at the shop. She parked her Jeep in the back and walked up front. She bundled up in her warm Sorel boots with her leggings tucked into warm wool socks. She zipped her puffy Patagonia coat all the way up to her chin and pulled her mittens snug. It was a chilly winter day, but nothing that would cause frostbite. She was a hearty Minnesotan. A casual winter stroll down Main Street would feel good.

Sometimes, especially during the holidays, Maggie liked to walk and just observe the sights of a small town. If anything was nostalgic at Christmas time, it was a town like Crosby, Minnesota. The Christmas classics could be heard on the speakers that connected to the tall street lights. *Silver Bells, Up on the Housetop* and songs from *The Nutcracker* were mixing with the sounds of town hubbub—honking horns, bells of business front doors jingling much like those on Maggie's door of the shop, semi truck's beeping sounds as they backed into allies to unload boxes of Christmas goods, a dog bark here and there and the occasional hello as Maggie passed other morning walkers. The snow shoveled into neat piles was lined between sidewalk and street. Maggie could hear a slight crunching sound under her boots as she walked due to business owners diligently salting the sidewalks.

Clem opened the front door to his small grocery store as Maggie walked by.

"Good morning to one of my favorite girls," he called.

She smiled.

"You say that to all the girls walking by don't you, Clem?"

He laughed.

"No, I do not. I like that you appear to be enjoying yourself this lovely morning, Mags. Sometimes, I still see contentment in the way you hold your face, or in your smile. Reminds me of years ago. I say to myself- there she is."

On most days this comment may have brought Maggie an ache in her chest and even a lump in her throat. But not today. She couldn't pinpoint why, but her dream of Samuel a few nights ago seemed to give her strength rather than the weakness she was so used to feeling. It had been so hard to wake up and realize it had been just a dream, as usual. But, it felt so real. She could almost still feel how smooth his freshly shaved cheeks had felt against the palms of her hands. His scent still lingered, a mix of her favorite Armani cologne, hand soap and a light mint smell on his breath from sucking on wintergreen Lifesavers all day. She still felt his loving stare, days after the dream, but wasn't sad. She welcomed the feeling.

Maggie brushed a dusting of snow from her hair when the wind had gusted briefly. She recalled thinking the dream, if described to someone, sounded like a scene from a sad love story. But she couldn't deny that it just felt different. So real and new and well, reviving to be honest.

Clem was right. Today she was feeling really good.

"Maggie, slow down."

She turned to see who was calling out her name.

He caught up to her, huffing and puffing a bit, as if he had run for two blocks, and maybe he had, after Maggie saw who it was and knew how far away his dental office was.

"My goodness Stuart, you surprised me. Ummm, are you ok?" She asked, trying to hide her smile.

He snickered a bit himself.

"I called your name a couple of times, but you were definitely day dreaming."

Another gust of wind blew through her hair, causing a few strands to catch on her eyelashes.

Stuart reached out to brush them from her face, but flinched and pulled back his hand, thinking better of it. He clearly didn't want to be too forward, but it felt natural.

Maggie didn't want to make for an awkward moment so instead she turned to keep walking toward *Cream and Sugar*.

"How about a cup of coffee? That's what I'm in search of," she casually suggested over her shoulder.

"That sounds great," Stuart replied as he zipped up his coat and started walking next to Maggie.

"Don't you love the feel of a small town at Christmas time? I know it isn't a macho thing to comment on, and let's be honest I'm not a macho guy anyway, but I have always loved how the town comes alive in December. It's like the business owners are in a friendly competition to see who can *deck the halls*, so to speak, the best. The holiday music is playing over the speakers in town and, I know I'm a dork, but the smell of butter cookies and nutty potica coming from *Pumpernickel House* and floating down the streets, makes me feel like a kid again."

Maggie felt warm and fuzzy after the description Stuart gave. Part of her wanted to reach out and tuck her arm through his as they walked. If they were starring in a *Hallmark Channel* movie, this would have been the obvious move, but they were not, and it just wasn't quite the time.

"Here we are. After you," Stuart offered, after opening up the large glass door to *Cream and Sugar*.

"Thank you, Sir." Maggie replied, politely.

Nora's coffee shop wasn't busy this morning and Maggie was a bit relieved. After a walk down Main Street and a coffee together at *Cream and Sugar*, the town gossip would be spreading.

As they walked up to order their drinks, Maggie's ease diminished immediately. Glancing at the stiletto clad woman entering the building, she realized herself and Stuart were about to have a very inquisitive patron waiting in line behind them.

Maggie removed her mittens and hat and tucked them into her coat pockets, suddenly feeling like someone had cranked up the thermostat. Stuart hadn't yet noticed the sound of clicking heels coming closer behind them.

Maggie thought, *who the hell wears stiletto heels in the snow anyway?*

The strong scent of her Chanel perfume was unmistakable, and Maggie noticed Stuart stuttering as he ordered a tall peppermint latte.

Despite his discomfort, he turned to Maggie and offered, "What will you have? It's my treat."

Maggie felt a little sorry for Caroline in that moment, a little guilty and a little embarrassed too. It was obvious to both Caroline and the young girl taking the drink order, that Maggie and Stuart were there together.

She cleared her throat, "Ahem, yes, I'll just have a regular drip coffee, please. With cream."

As they waited at the end of the counter, all three of them, Caroline finally was the brave one to break the silence.

"Stuart, are you able to join our group this Friday evening for the wine tasting fundraiser? You had said you were in full support of the cause," Caroline said while she clicked her red nails on her cell phone.

Stuart's forehead turned into a crease and then a question in his eyes. He glanced at Maggie and scrunched his shoulders as if to say, "I don't know what she's talking about."

Caroline continued.

"I'll put you down as a sponsor. We really appreciate the support. Don't forget, December 14th, out at Lonesome Road Lodge."

Caroline grabbed her sugar free, skim milk latte out of the hands of the young barista faster than she could say the name on the order. Stuart and Maggie watched as she raced out the door, confused but not overly surprised.

"Thank you," Maggie said, taking their coffees from the girl at the counter. She turned to Stuart. "Do you still not have a clue what cause you just signed up as a sponsor for?"

"Honestly, I really am trying to recall." He sipped on his peppermint latte and looked to be thinking hard for a moment. "Well, I'm stumped. I will have to run it by the girls at the office today and see if they remember me signing up for something. Absolutely, no disrespect to the cause in which Caroline speaks, but there just is always something and I do, occasionally, lose track."

Maggie laughed, as they began to walk. "Ya know, you are human. That's ok. I forget things all of the time. I have sticky notes to remember to read my sticky notes."

Stuart smiled.

As they arrived at *The Maple Leaf,* Maggie stopped.

"This is me. Thanks for the coffee, Stuart. And for the company on my stroll."

"It was my pleasure," he replied, and with that he continued walking down the sidewalk.

Maggie stood and watched him until he turned the corner.

CHAPTER 23

As the week ticked on, Maggie started prepping the little room in the back of her shop to make it more comfortable for the babies while Flynn and Rose were out of town for a few days. She was both excited and a little anxious to babysit Jade and Sophia. Of course she had gotten to know them as she and Rose grew to be best friends, but she still had very little experience with infants and she wasn't their mama. Sometimes that is all a little one wants and they were pretty good at letting you know it too. Maggie, however, made an extra effort to act absolutely relaxed and confident about the whole plan, for Rose. As a new mom, she was having a hard time leaving the girls, despite Flynn's carefully laid plans.

Maggie brought in a beautiful wooden rocking chair she had from home. She set that in the corner of the room, next to a small table with a lamp set on top. The window to her left luckily had a shade she could pull down when the girls were napping. Maggie had a small refrigerator and microwave in the storage room also, so she could make bottles and warm up baby food. Flynn and Rose would be bringing the Jumparoos and Pack n Plays. Maggie kept a few simple toys in a basket in the corner of the store for bored kids to play with as their mothers shopped. So, she could grab a few of those if the girls wanted to stretch out on a large quilt and play.

Jade and Sophia became more and more inquisitive as the days went on. Though Maggie felt a tiny ache in her heart every time she looked at their perfect little faces, she also loved having the chance to enjoy babies. For someone who had yearned for a child, never could keep one and had lost the slim chance of conceiving once her husband died—the beauty in such a simple little person was never lost on Maggie. Babies cried, yes. They pooped, yes. They took a lot of tending and patience, of course. But they were also learning something new every day. They smiled at familiar faces with sheer joy. Their perfect little chubby hands reaching out for a toy, or their mother's face was priceless. The feather light curls of hair that bunched above two little pink ears were angelic.

Maggie sighed. She folded a couple of small towels to use as burping cloths and set them on the table next to the rocking chair. Then turning off the light, she walked out of the room and shut the door.

"Maggie? Dear, are you here today?"

"Oh, goodness Mabel. You surprised me. I didn't hear you come in!"

"I'm sorry sweetheart. I wasn't trying to be sneaky," Mabel apologized.

"You weren't trying to sneak in, but you did bring me a little surprise, it looks like huh?" Maggie teased as she glanced down at something in Mabel's hands.

"Well certainly I did. We made another one of your favorites today and I told Henry I had to run a plate over to Maggie. Here you go—Swedish Kringle."

"Mabel, with you and Henry, I can't keep on a diet to save my life. Who can resist?"

Maggie peeled back the tin foil and smelled the almond extract that was baked into each layer including the icing drizzled on top. Per *Pumpernickel* tradition, sliced almonds and chopped candied cherries decorated the top.

Maggie set the plate down and gave little old Mabel a big hug.

"Thank you, Mabel. You're too good to me."

Mabel held Maggie's hand in both of hers, patting it softly.

"We have known you and Samuel for many years and I know this time of year is the toughest. You're like family, Maggie. We are always right next door. And I've found baked goods at least give people a smile, even if they can't heal every wound. With time and the occasional sweet roll, life will be wonderful again, someday."

Mabel let go of Maggie's hand before her lip began to quiver.

"Ok. I am needed back at the bakery. You enjoy your Kringle, dear. Goodbye."

Maggie sat down on a nearby dining room chair and looked at her Christmas treat sitting on the table in front of her and to her surprise, she smiled instead of cried. The thought of Samuel gave her warm comfort like a hug instead of the all too familiar stab in the heart. She wondered, is this what the healing process was? She still had some nightmares, still woke up crying with a struggle to catch her breath from time to time. But this? This was new. She liked being able to remember her loving, caring and fun husband and the memories they had shared without immediately trying to block them out for fear of falling deep into an abyss of depression and emotional exhaustion.

She wondered if the dream she had had of Samuel a couple weeks ago had something to do with it. The dream had felt more real than anything she had been living right now, day to day. More real and palpable than this dish with Maggie's favorite childhood Christmas dessert sitting upon it right in front of her.

Samuel had said to her as she held his perfect face in her hands, "Find Faith". She heard of people telling family members to have faith or keep the faith, but it was conceivable that she had none when it involved getting over Samuel. But, since his visit, or what absolutely felt like a visit, it had seemed her faith was strengthening.

What was even more astounding is that she felt open to the thought of dating Stuart, or at least giving herself permission to be his friend without a complete overtaking of guilt.

It was new. It was unnerving. But she had no doubt that Samuel was behind the feeling of contentment she suddenly felt.

Maggie pulled the tin foil up and peeled it back from the plate. She picked up a square of Kringle and took a small bite. It was a bite of

Christmases gone by—sweet and fleeting, but with a joy that nothing could ever replace.

Samuel too, for Maggie, was a sweet and fleeting joy in her life.

One that nothing or no one could ever truly replace.

CHAPTER 24

"Ok Maggie, Jade's favorite blanket is this lavender one with the little yellow moons on it. Sophia prefers the quilted pink one with a fringe. I know they are babies, but they are two different little humans. They have their own likes and dislikes, their own personalities and their own routines. Flynn, wouldn't you agree? It's true, look at how Sophia is clenching on to that blankie," Rose commented, anxiously.

Flynn glanced at Maggie with a sympathetic look in his eyes. For his wife or for Maggie, she couldn't decide.

"Ok, Rosebud, babe—look at the girls sitting on this puffy quilt Maggie has laid out for them with one of every kind of toy you can think of. She has spent many hours with you and the babies these last months. They know Maggie well. It is going to be just fine."

Maggie felt obliged to chime in. .

"Well yes, of course. In fact Rose, we are going to have a great time. I've only ever had smiles and giggles from the both of them when they sit on my lap. Flynn is right, they know me and my friend—it will be ok."

Rose crouched down next to Jade and Sophia who were rolling around and kicking their legs in the air like there wasn't a care in the world.

"Oh wow. I am acting more like a baby than my babies laying in front of me aren't I?" Rose groaned.

Then bravely grabbing Flynn's arm she headed for the door.

"Ok, let's go. Maggie, thank you so much for taking them. You have our phone numbers, my mom's cell phone and the Inn's number. Call for any reason."

Flynn, taking advantage of Rose's sudden willingness to leave, waved a quick goodbye to Maggie and escorted his wife out the front door.

Maggie turned to her new mini tenants and marveled at how their every little move was intentional and focused. Again, she couldn't keep the admiration she had at bay when she watched these perfect tiny humans. It was always like witnessing a miracle, minute by minute, day to day.

She quietly and gently sat down on the corner of the blanket and picked up one of her old little golden books and began to read. She had seen Marie do this many mornings when Rose and Lucille were serving breakfast at the Inn and knew the girls were comforted by it. She had enjoyed it as a child too. Her mom had read to her every night before bed. Maggie had saved many of her favorites.

"Once upon a time…" she began. Before three pages had been read, both girls were sleeping soundly. Maggie thought it to be the wisest decision to not move them, but to cover them each with their favorite blanket (as described by Rose) and let them nap on the quilt. She could leave the door cracked open a bit and would hear them if they woke up.

It was a cold, overcast day outside and a warm and cozy one inside the shop. As she did each morning, Maggie turned on her Christmas playlist to lend to the mood. Most of her Christmas decor had already been put up in front of the windows and throughout the store. She did have a few boxes of brand new inventory she still needed to go through and decide where to display those items. Grabbing one of the boxes from behind the counter she yanked off the tape and folded open the flaps. Pulling off the generous layers of bubble wrap she saw what was inside and gasped with excitement. Maggie reached in and grabbed a small six inch flat box with a picture on the front of a gold candelabra stand. This unique type of stand held four small finger size candles and balancing above on an elaborate post in the middle was a spinning carousel of sorts with brass angels. There were two dome shaped chimes just below. When Maggie was growing up, her grandmother pulled one of these out of storage every year during the holidays. She called it a Lichter-Glocken-Spiel, a tradition she had brought from Sweden. Maggie remembered thinking it was pure magic as a child. Granny would help her very carefully put the glockenspiel together and then she would light the candles. Maggie would watch carefully and just about the time her patience would start to dwindle, the most amazing thing would happen. The angels would start spinning on their little carousel and as that happened the trumpets they were holding would tap the chimes and the ding, ding, ding could be heard. It was a magical moment that she still held close to her heart all these years later.

Looking at the box Maggie smiled and ran her hand across the picture of the child looking at the beautiful sight in front of them with the same look of awe she had had years ago. She decided that the perfect place to display the glockenspiels was out by the Christmas tree in front so they wouldn't be missed by shoppers walking by outside.

Before doing so, she stood up and walked to the room where Jade and Sophia were napping. Quietly, she peeked in and listened. Both little babies laid still under their blankets, fast asleep. Maggie snuck back out and shut the door lightly again.

"Ok, let's go put these pretty things out by the window, shall we Muffin?" she called over her shoulder to her puffy feline friend, while carrying the box around tables and cabinets. She waited a moment and heard his little pitter patter of paws following her.

"I sure have a good helper here, don't I?" She laughed as Muffin caught up and rubbed against her leg.

Maggie spent the next thirty minutes or so carefully stacking and arranging the glockenspiel kits on shelves and around the base of the Christmas tree like gifts. She opened the other two boxes which contained more ornaments as well as vintage looking gift wrap, bows and gift tags. She moved a favorite old chest to the display window where she threw the rolls of wrapping paper and bows inside. The gift tags she fanned out neatly on a wooden chair sitting nearby. Standing back and looking at her work, though a pleasant, welcoming scene, it needed something more. There was the tree, the glockenspiels placed underneath and sitting here and there. Antique glass ornaments hung on the tree and glistened on shelves in clear glass jars. The chest was a perfect touch with gold and red wrapping paper peeking out. She stacked a few oversized knit blankets here and there to give a warm feeling. Sitting down on the floor next to the chest, she thought *This scene is missing a fireplace.* How quaint and homey would it be to add one. Naturally and logistically a true fireplace with a hearth and chimney couldn't be added, but how about one of those small electric ones? You could find those online now. They were reasonably priced and the flame looked almost real in most of them, at least enough to lend to the "I'll be home for Christmas" vibe she was striving to present here.

Looking at Muffin curled up comfortably on the gift tags she neatly arranged on the chair, Maggie rolled her eyes.

"Wouldn't that pile of blankets over there be more comfortable? It certainly would have been preferred by me, Muffin. Silly cat." Maggie stood up and started walking toward the counter in the back where she had left her cell phone.

"I am on a mission to find a small electric fireplace. Do you think Amazon has those, Muffin?" Maggie yelled behind her.

It startled Maggie when she heard a tiny cry from the back room. She was so engrossed in her decorating, that she almost forgot to check on the babies.

Another cry followed.

Maggie stood up, yelling, "I'm coming girls!" as if the promise would make them pause their whimpers.

She pushed open the door and by habit flicked the light switch. The intense bright light caused Jade and Sophia to become scared and both babies started whaling at a higher pitch.

"Oh, I'm so sorry little ones. Here, I'll turn on the lamp."

Maggie pulled the little chain hanging under the lamp shade and the soft light warmed the room. After switching off the obnoxious spot light up above, she reached down and picked up Sophia. Both she and her sister, Jade, continued their unwavering screams without any sign of easing them.

Maggie tried to comfort Sophia first, sway and bounce and rock her from side to side. Though it seemed to work a little at first, Jade was becoming more and more hysterical. Setting Sophia back down, Maggie decided to go prepare a couple of bottles for the girls. She remembered Rose had said they were now able to hold their bottles themselves and the warm milk and comforting routine may soothe them and settle them down. Afterall, this was a new, strange place to them.

Maggie was just finishing up warming the second bottle when she heard the bells on her front door jingle. She felt a tiny bead of sweat begin to form at her hairline.

Maybe I wasn't prepared for this as much as I thought I was, she suddenly thought, becoming a touch overwhelmed.

"Maggie? Are you here? I am hoping so, cuz I hear tiny cries coming from somewhere and I'm hoping there is an adult tending to them?"

She heard Stuart's voice and became mortified.

This is too embarrassing. How am I going to resolve this situation while appearing to be calmly in control? she asked herself. Deciding on just going for the raw and honest approach she poked her head out from the storage room.

"Stuart! Help! I am babysitting Rose and Flynn's twins and they woke up from their naps and are a tad unhappy. I assume they are wondering where the hell they are! Poor things."

"Hmmm, are you referring to the deafening sound I hear? I hadn't noticed, really."

"Hey! No time for jokes. Here, take a bottle!" Maggie said, throwing one to Stuart. "This way."

He followed her to the back room where the girls were still crying and kicking their legs in the air in preparation for a full blown temper tantrum.

"Here, it's ok, it's ok. Come Stuart, let's sit down close to them and try a softer approach." Maggie advised.

Stuart followed suit, each of them speaking quietly to the babies and handing them their bottles. Maggie was so hopeful all would be ok, but she soon found out that Jade and Sophia had become too worked up to even grip their bottles and Maggie feared that even if she tried feeding them they would choke on the milk for lack of letting up on their screams. She began to feel a panic welling up in her chest. Stuart tried to speak softly to the girls and occasionally would offer the same tone to Maggie in the form of encouraging words. They each, again, attempted picking up the babies, but this only amplified their distress, and now the babies' cries had transformed into a mad and frustrated scream.

Finally when Maggie's eyes began to gloss over with tears of her own, she thought of a ridiculous idea.

What's the harm in trying? I was entranced watching it when I was little. Maybe even babies will notice the magic, she thought.

Then turning to Stuart, she gave orders.

"Ok, grab a baby and follow me Stuart!"

He softly picked up Jade as Maggie scooped up Sophia and along with their favorite blankets and bottles, walked out to the display window. Maggie pointed to the Windsor chair next to a small side table cuddled close to the Christmas tree scene she had created earlier when the shop was much quieter. Stuart understood and sat down. She plopped Sophia on his other knee next to her sister. Both babies looked confused and were still working hard on showing their displeasure. Stuart too was wondering about the wonderful plan Maggie suddenly had.

She pulled out a small flat box from the shelf behind her and quickly started assembling some sort of candle set? He wasn't sure. Then Maggie grabbed a box of matches from behind a glass jar of ornaments and lit one. Just the bright flame made the babies settle momentarily, but after the candles were lit, slowly the sobs started again.

"Maggie, this is a pretty Christmas decoration, but do you think they are going to care a whole lot?" Stuart quietly asked.

"Probably not, but it's worth a try. It's a magic that I was mesmerized by when I was little. Was I a baby? No, but this is our last chance before I call Rose and ask her what to do."

Stuart could see Maggie's flush cheeks and the slight shake in her hand as she blew out the match, and decided he would go with the flow.

After several very trying moments, the brass angels perched on the stand just above the candles and two dome shaped chimes, started spinning in carousel fashion, and then the trumpets they held began to tap the chimes creating a pleasing bell sound. Suddenly, somehow, the bell sounds were all that could be heard besides the occasional sniffle.

Maggie looked across the table where she had set up the glockenspiel and saw two tiny pink faces, wet with tears and perspiration, completely entranced, their round little eyes barely allowing a blink. Something in the movement, the shine of the candlelight on the brass and the melodic ting of the chimes, caused these two sweet little people to forget why they had been so incredibly upset. They stared. Their little chests would rise and fall with each soft breath. Occasionally they would wiggle their tiny fingers or glance away for a split second, but it was clear they had both calmed down and were, for the moment, content.

Maggie smiled and couldn't help appreciating the touching scene in front of her. Stuart sitting so very still, with identical twin baby girls cozy on his lap, all staring at the glockenspiel do its magic. She didn't know if it would be ok, but she took the chance. Grabbing her cell phone from her back pocket, she turned off the flash and snapped a quick picture. Stuart looked up and winked.

Maggie whispered, "Let's try to give them their bottles now that they are settled down."

She picked up Jade from his lap, handed him a bottle for Sophia and then she went and sat down on a nearby armchair. After she and Stuart gave it another try, the girls both realized how thirsty they had become and took their bottles happily.

Maggie sat back, relaxing in the chair while cradling Jade in her arms. Every once in a while she'd pull her little lips off the nipple of the bottle to catch another glimpse of the glockenspiel, but would turn back suddenly to continue drinking.

Maggie looked over at Stuart and was impressed by how comfortable he looked holding Sophia. She, too, was stealing the occasional glance of the shimmering magic in front of her.

"Stuart," Maggie said quietly.

His eyes shot up from where he was staring at the flame of the candles.

"Yea? What's up?"

Maggie's lips turned up into a little grin.

"Nothing. Just...thank you for showing up."

"Oh, well I didn't have a clue you were in need of an assistant babysitter, but I'm always happy to help out."

Maggie laughed softly.

She didn't know if she wanted him to know yet that when she said thank you for showing up, she hadn't meant just tonight.

CHAPTER 25

"Sanchez, I don't want to use foul language in front of the ladies, but you are full of blankety blank," Flynn accused jokingly while the group of friends and new acquaintances laughed. "You could not bench press three hundred pounds while we were serving."

"Hell I couldn't Mitchell. We were lifting every day. I'm short and stocky. All my muscle sits up top," Sanchez argued, throwing a kernel of popcorn across the table at his buddy.

"You both are liars! I was the strong one, and the toughest I might add. I took a bullet even," Collins bragged. But then, looking down at his wife's weakening smile, he decided to change the subject. War talk certainly didn't make for light conversation and was a subject that threatened the cheerful tone of the evening.

"Well, anyway, let me grab you ladies another glass of wine. Kara, do you want to replenish the bowls of popcorn?"

Collins and his wife, Kara, stood up and excused themselves from the table and walked into the kitchen. Flynn reached over and held Rose's hand.

Leaning closer, he whispered, "Are you having a good time, Rosebud? Do you like Kara and Isabel?"

Rose squeezed his hand back.

"I am. And I do. But, do you think the girls are doing ok Hon.? I can't help but wonder."

"I know. I was thinking the same. Why don't you go give Maggie a quick call? You'll feel better and be able to enjoy the rest of the night," Flynn suggested.

"Ya think that would be ok?" Rose replied.

Flynn laughed.

"They are your children, Rosebud. You can call thirty times in a row if you want to. Though, our babysitters may never feel obliged to have them again after that."

"Ok, fine. I'm going to run up to our room quickly then. Be right back."

Rose kissed Flynn's cheek and headed upstairs to call home.

While Rose was upstairs Collins and Kara returned with another bottle of chardonnay and one of merlot, as well as bowls of popcorn and a tray of cheeses and sliced meats. Rose had made a pan of fudge and had set a tray in the middle of the table earlier to share.

"Here we are. Rose, Chardonnay or Merl–? Oh, ooops, where did she go?" Collins asked Flynn.

Flynn smiled.

"Well, she is a little worried about the babies. We haven't left Jade and Sophia overnight just yet. I could tell she wanted to call home and check on them, so I told her there was no harm in doing so."

"Awww, I don't blame her. Even with our kids being ages four and two and at Grandma's, we still wonder how they are doing overnight," Kara added.

"Well, Rose has become good friends with a gal she met in Crosby, Maggie Ollweyes. She owns a shop on Main Street — home decorations and stuff. But, anyway that is who the babies are with at least for the time being. Rose's parents will be picking them up later tonight."

"That's great, man. I'm glad you two are settling into the new town and making friends," Sanchez commented.

"Yea, it's good. In fact, Maggie's husband was in the Army and stationed over in Afghanistan during the time us three were, which was a weird coincidence. So, the two have bonded over that too I guess. Just the

Army wife thing and being left behind and such."

Collins finished filling Isabel's glass with wine and looked at Flynn.

"*Was* in the Army? Did he retire or? I hate to ask…"

Flynn glanced at both Isabel and Kara sitting, listening intently, and felt a jolt of painful respect for these women who were left behind wondering if their husbands might never return to them. For Maggie, that nightmare came to be.

Flynn fidgeted.

"Well, he didn't come home unfortunately. As we say, he made the ultimate sacrifice that day."

Without a need for prompting, naturally, the group sat in silence with respect for their fallen brother.

Sanchez broke the silence finally.

"What was his name, Mitchell?"

Flynn looked up, thinking for a moment.

"Umm, Samuel. Samuel Ollweyes."

Flynn noticed Sanchez glanced at Collins for a brief moment with a puzzled look of recognition, but seemed to want to hide the reaction quickly.

"Well, here's to Samuel Ollweyes. We honor you, brother," he said and raised his glass in a toast. Everyone around the table did the same and took a sip in quiet respect of Maggie's husband.

Rose soon came down the stairs with a content smile on her face.

Flynn could tell that she had received the news she was hoping to hear from Maggie and he too felt relief. Both that his sweet girls were well taken care of and that Rose hadn't returned until the talk of Samuel had ended.

Rose took a long, relaxed drink of her Chardonnay and sat down, ready for some adult conversation. Knowing now that Jade and Sophia were happy, sleepy and had full bellies made her feel like she could finally allow herself to enjoy the night.

"So, Flynn, what's this 6 5 4 game you said we were gonna play?" Rose asked, winking at her husband.

Collins stood up and yelled.

"Thank you Rose! I had forgotten about that! I'll grab the dice. Prepare to lose some moola y'all!"

Everyone laughed and started digging out loose change, but Flynn suddenly had a strange feeling in his stomach. Not necessarily a bad feeling just yet, but after seeing the way Sanchez shot a glance at Collins after hearing Samuel's full name, Flynn had an inclination they had known him or at least had known *of* him.

And now, he wasn't sure how to deal with it.

CHAPTER 26

Evie had invited Maggie over for dinner on Sunday after they had picked the babies up from her shop. It was the last night before Rose and Flynn returned and Evie said Maggie deserved to eat a meal she didn't have to cook herself and then just get home and relax.

Grateful for the offer, Maggie obliged.

Maggie sat at the kitchen table in Rose's kitchen bouncing Sophia on her knee while Philip held Jade as she started nodding off to sleep. Evie had told Maggie that Jade hadn't slept well the night before and was bound to fall asleep early tonight. Clearly, she was spot on.

Evie had pulled out a shepherd's pie from the oven that was filling the room with a tantalizing scent. If Maggie was being honest, she couldn't recall ever having tried it, but what could be bad about meat and potatoes mixed into one warm and hearty winter dish?

"Can I help you, Evie?" Maggie offered.

"No, no dear. You have your hands full with my granddaughter," Evie replied, smiling with total admiration at the baby Maggie was holding. "I've got this all under control. This is an easy dinner anyway. Nothing fancy I'm afraid."

"Oh, well it smells delicious. I see where Rose gets her talents as a chef," Maggie complimented.

Philip piped up from across the table.

"What makes you think it isn't me?"

Evie burst out laughing from where she stood at the counter. Maggie smiled.

"Oh, ok. I will admit, if anyone is a better cook than my daughter, it's

123

her mother," Philip admitted.

Evie brought the pie over to the table and set it on top of a hot pad, then grabbed a tossed salad and a sliced loaf of bread and set both down as well.

"Ok, Philip, give me little Jade. She's had it. I'm going to bring her up to bed. Maggie, you can set Sophia in her high chair while we eat dinner. She's fine sucking on her pacifier for now. Her head will be bobbing too before long."

Evie softly took Jade from her husband's arms and left the room. Maggie hadn't had many conversations with Philip in the short time they had been acquainted, so the silence was a bit awkward at first. She stood up and set Sophia in her high chair and looked around for her little pink pacifier.

"Oh, here it is," Philip said grabbing the pink pacifier off the counter and handing it to Maggie.

"Here you are, little girl," she said, gently putting it in Sophia's mouth. Then taking her seat, she offered, "Can I scoop you up a piece of this lovely looking Shepherd's Pie, Philip?"

"Yes, indeed, I am starving. Thank you, Maggie."

Maggie buttered a slice of bread and added a portion of salad to her plate and both began to eat. Finally Evie returned.

"Ok, she is out like a light. Awww, Sophia, like I said, you're getting sleepy too aren't you?"

Maggie enjoyed the meal Evie had prepared and had a light conversation with Rose's kind parents. Like Rose and Flynn, they were good hearted people.

As Maggie drove away, with leftovers sitting in the passenger's seat, she felt grateful for having these new people in her life.

CHAPTER 27

Rose, Isabel and Kara sipped on warm cups of coffee in the living room by the fireplace while their husbands were outside snowshoeing on the trails nearby. The guys had invited their wives, but the temps had dipped a bit overnight and none of the ladies sounded overly keen on the idea. Oversized blankets, hallmark movies and hazelnut coffee was far more appealing to them all. The smoky scent of the burning logs in the fireplace pairing with the snowy picturesque scene outside made for a postcard kind of day.

Rose watched the tv screen switch from movie to movie as Kara decided on which holiday "rom com" they would watch. She sipped the nutty, rich liquid in her mug and sighed with an utter relaxation she hadn't thought she could obtain on this vacation. It had been more difficult than she thought, leaving the girls. So much so, that when she started to cry on the first turn out of town, Flynn had offered to go home and cancel the whole trip. But, Rose knew there had to be a first time eventually. Though she missed her baby girls, it had been a wonderful weekend. And as Flynn had promised, she too felt like she had made some lifelong friends.

Peering out the large window of the Collins's cabin, Rose could see the guys in the distance snowshoeing their way to the beginning of a trail that winded through the trees. She couldn't help but notice the extreme beauty here in Manitoba, Canada. Much like Minnesota, it had the tall snow covered pines and iced over lakes, but it seemed even more untouched, more untamed, besides this cabin, it looked uninhabited. At least the forest in which they were encompassed by sure did. Rose figured there was a city somewhere near, but she didn't really even know exactly where they were in Manitoba. Off the beaten path, that she was certain of.

She wondered what Flynn and his friends were talking about out there, or if it was just quiet focus as they traipsed through the snow.

"Ugh, as usual I can't find anything. Should we watch *Chopped, Holiday Edition* instead? I love this show," Kara suggested, finally.

Isabel and Rose gave her a thumbs up and they began watching the judges sample Christmas themed concoctions.

Flynn followed the trail a couple yards behind Collins and Sanchez was a few behind him. There was a bite in the air forming little frozen crystals on his eyebrows and lashes. When they had started their trek out into the woods, Flynn realized he had been freezing, but snowshoeing was a work out and soon he had hardly noticed the chill outside.

He noticed the beauty on the trails as they weaved through the forest. The clean white snow sparkled when the sun peeked out from behind the clouds casting large Norway pine shadows across their path. From time to time a squirrel would skitter past and hide behind the remnants of a fallen oak. And it was quiet. So beautifully silent. So much so that the only sounds he could hear were the crunching of snow and the pattern of his breathing in and out. The silence did cause him to get lost in his thoughts, particularly regarding the conversation they had briefly two nights ago about Samuel Ollweyes. It had been such a brief glance Sanchez had given Collins, that for the last two days Flynn was wondering if he was making something out of nothing, but he realized he knew these guys. They had to read each other's looks, gestures, body language when they were serving together. At times that is what they relied on as communication in very dangerous situations.

So, as much as Flynn had questioned himself, he knew now, especially out here in the lonesome, desolate wild, he knew there was something his friends weren't telling him. Finally, after they had journeyed down the trails for an hour, Flynn decided he had to just ask his friends what and if they knew anything about Maggie's husband, Samuel. Perhaps it had been only gossip or hearsay, but he needed to know something. He wouldn't feel right not at least asking.

"Ok brothers, let's take a granola bar break shall we?" he suggested casually.

CHAPTER 28

Maggie kneeled down next to the large flower pots she had purchased from the local greenhouse along with several flats of her favorite plants. Sitting next to her were bags of potting soil and her watering can full to the brim. She loved spring. It smelled of clean rain, rich soil and freshly cut grass. There was hardly a moment, even at 8:00 at night when the sun was ready to set, that the tweeting and songs of birds couldn't be heard. There was new life, fresh starts, beauty being born from every angle you looked.

She closed her eyes and breathed in a cool cleansing breath of fresh May air. Then, going back to her task at hand she picked up a container of alyssum. The tiny white, happy looking blooms were her favorite. Digging small holes in the soil she had dumped into her large pots, she dropped the alyssum plants in and lightly packed the dirt around them, followed by a sprinkle of water. Bright purple petunias followed and a lime green splash of sweet potato vine for contrast. Maggie decided she had chosen a good combo this year.

After planting her pots, the rock garden in front of the deck and the raised bed around the light post, she decided to call it a day, at least for outside work. She gathered the empty flat cardboard boxes, plastic pots, and deadhead leaves and flowers and tossed them in the garbage can outside. Before going inside Maggie tossed her dirty garden gloves through the garage window, deciding she would deal with them later. A warm shower sounded good.

As she opened up the screen door to go inside the house she heard the sound of crunching pebbles under moving tires and turned to see Samuel's truck turning the corner into their driveway.

Maggie smiled. *He's home early today. Great, I can show him what I planted and we can throw those pork chops on the grill we purchased Saturday at the farmer's market,* she thought.

Samuel honked as he pulled his Chevy pickup into the garage. Maggie waved and walked closer. She still got excited when she saw his truck coming down the driveway. After several years of being a couple, many of them as a married couple, Maggie *still* noticed the butterflies in her stomach when Samuel was around. The biggest thing was the happiness in his eyes when he smiled at her- genuine, honest and just "in love" basically. And they were, no doubt about it. Still.

"Hey Sweetheart. Aren't you a beauty today!" Samuel called to his wife as she met him outside the garage.

"Oh yea. Sweaty, stringy hair pulled back into a ponytail, dirt crusted to my knee caps and your stained Army t-shirt! I am ready for the red carpet, babe," Maggie laughed.

"Ah huh. That's the way I like it. Real. My wife. My loving, perfect wife—dirt and all," Samuel said, scooping her up in his arms. He opened the front door with one hand and carried her in, slipping off his shoes in a quick motion. They both were in need of a shower and that's where he was headed.

Maggie woke with tears already dripping on her pillow. She rolled over and grabbed a tissue from the nightstand and blew her nose. She tossed the crumpled up ball on the floor, not caring where it landed for the time being.

"Samuel, I love you, but it would be much easier to *find faith* as you say in my dreams, if you didn't visit them so much. By finding faith I assume you mean finding the faith to move on and have hope in the future, my future. Even find love again. Am I on the right track here? It's just so, so hard when you visit me in my dreams and I feel you like you are right there in my arms. I used to feel like those were little gifts from God. A brief visit from one of his angels so that I can experience the love we had if only for a moment. But now, I—I just can't move on if you keep coming back."

Maggie sat up staring at the framed photos that still sat on her dresser and the wall. She needed to *help* herself move on. She needed to pack away the memories. It was time.

How though? Wrap Samuel's face in bubble wrap and stack in boxes? She felt her eyes begin to gloss over again, just thinking of it. Then she heard his voice in her head.

Maggie, Find Faith. You can do it. I will help you along the way. Find the strength to do so.

With that Maggie let her tears fall as she gathered the photos from her dresser and the shelf above their bed and carried them downstairs in search of a storage box.

CHAPTER 29

On the ride home from Manitoba, Rose was so excited to see Jade and Sophia she could hardly stop talking. They had been driving since 8:00 that morning after having coffee and bagels with Flynn's friends. Rose agreed she was glad they had taken the trip and was happy to have met the Collins's and Sanchez', but she sure was eager to get home.

"So, did you and your buddies get some good bonding in, Flynn?" Rose asked.

"Yea, I'd say so. It was a good time. I had missed those guys. I hope we can do it again sometime. Maybe they all could come stay at the Inn one weekend when it's a slower time of year," Flynn suggested.

"Oh, that would be great. Really, why don't they all bring their kids the next time? We can make it a family thing. Games, pizza, trips to the candy store and park. Why not?" Rose answered, liking the idea.

Flynn patted her hand as they continued on the drive. It would be a few hours yet before they reached Crosby and *Simpler Times*. Both sat in silence as they wondered how everyone fared in their absence. It was a lot to ask of friends and family to take two babies and keep an Inn running. But taking a vacation, even a three day one, had done them well.

"Hon, I'm going to close my eyes for a bit, if you don't mind, I didn't sleep very well last night. The wind was blowing so loudly out our window and I kept having uneasy dreams. But I don't want you to get drowsy without someone to talk to, either," Rose said.

Flynn seemed to hardly notice what she had said, but replied, "Yes, no worries. I will be fine."

Rose looked at him for a few seconds, wondering if he seemed a bit off, but then laid back brushing the thought away. As she slowly dozed off, Flynn took his hand from hers and gripped the steering wheel with both hands trying to focus on the road and not what was stirring in his brain. He had questioned Collins and Sanchez about the look they had shared when the group had been discussing Samuel Ollweyes two nights prior. He had called them out saying he knew their "looks" and he wanted to hear what they knew about his friend's husband. Finally, Collins and Sanchez had plopped down in a snowbank next to Flynn and filled him in on what they knew or what they had heard, rather. Flynn thought back to yesterday, about exactly twenty-four hours ago, while they were on the snowshoeing trail.

"Ok, let's take a break and let our burning calf muscles relax a bit huh?" Flynn suggested, trying to seem aloof.

"Oh man, yea, I was hoping someone would ask before I finally caved," Sanchez said, huffing and puffing. He took his water bottle from his pack and drained half of the water inside.

"Ahh, you two. It's like you don't get any physical activity. What happened to ya?" Collins laughed as he sat down on a large boulder peeking out of the snow.

Sanchez stood up to sock his friend in the shoulder, when Flynn piped up.

"Ok, listen guys. I didn't need a break, necessarily. I mean I'm not used to snowshoeing, but was I dying? No."

Flynn ripped open a raisin granola bar and bit off a corner, chewing slowly, stalling perhaps.

"The truth is. I know you two. We were trained to know each other's warning signs. Looks, gestures, movements. For God's sake, it helped save our lives a couple of times over there." He took off his hat and ran a nervous hand through his hair, still waiting for the words. He wanted to know what they were keeping from him, but at the same time wasn't sure what to do with the information.

Collins caved before Flynn could get the words out.

"Mitchell, the truth is—yes, we heard some things when we were all stationed in Afghanistan about your friend's husband, Samuel Ollweyes."

Flynn looked up, relieved that they also could read him too.

Sanchez looked at both of his buddies and taking one more swig from his water bottle he began to speak.

"So, we had heard that Samuel's truck hit an ERW and exploded, unfortunately leaving no survivors. Or maybe fortunately, depending on how you look at it. Had you managed to survive the detonation of a landmine, you wouldn't be in good shape, I'll tell you that. Either way man, a tragic loss."

Flynn cut in.

"Well, we kind of already knew that he had died instantly, no survivors, the whole thing. Maggie was told such."

"Well, yes. That isn't exactly the information we were holding back. There's more." Collins replied, looking at Sanchez to continue on with his story.

"Remember after Collins had been wounded he spent several weeks in a small hospital not far from base and you and I, Marty and a few others, including Captain Silva took turns visiting him?" Sanchez began.

"Yes, of course I remember." Flynn answered.

Collins stared for a moment across a snow white field, no doubt remembering every detail himself, from a far more frightening perspective, however.

"Oh, on one of my visit days, I was sitting in the four chair waiting room, well you know—waiting for the lady at the front counter to give me the ok to head down the hall to Collins's room. While I waited for, oh, 5, maybe 10 minutes, a soldier I'd say ten years older than me came in. He gave his name to the receptionist at the counter, Samuel Ollweyes. The name stuck with me cuz at the time I heard it like he was telling the receptionist that he wants to be called Samuel always, as in never Sam or anything else, just always Samuel. Then I realized his last name just sounded the same."

"Sanchez, can we get to the guts of the story, please?" Flynn asked, trying to keep his increasing impatience out of his tone.

"Yea, ok. He told her he was there to see a woman named Zahra something. I guess I didn't think much of it at that moment, but a week or two later, I was there again and when I walked past one of the rooms just down a few from Collins's room I saw him sitting at the side of a hospital bed looking down at a beautiful woman and he was holding her hand. I thought it a little strange, well I guess to be honest, a bit shocking. Here he was in his US Army fatigues holding the hand of, what appeared to be, an Afghan woman. Even with her eyes closed and her head heavily wrapped with bandages, it was clear she was an exceptionally attractive woman. What also was clear to me in that quick instant I let myself look in on their private moment, was that Sergeant First Class Samuel Ollweyes was heartbroken."

Flynn wasn't sure what to make of the information he had just heard. Obviously, US soldiers deployed to Afghanistan carried absolutely no ill will toward any of the civilians or even toward the Taliban on a man to man, personal level. They were there to do a duty, serve when and where they were instructed. The soldiers trusted in the instructions so completely that they would gladly give their lives.

It was rare, but conceivable that a soldier, maybe having been stationed for several months, could fall in love and have some sort of relationship with a woman from Afghanistan. But Samuel? Flynn recalled hearing his name while stationed in Afghanistan himself, but he had never met him. His judgment was purely coming from the admiration of his kind and beautiful wife, Maggie.

"I, I guess I'm not sure how to respond to this, or what to do with it?" Flynn stuttered.

"Look Mitchell, I know it puts you in a tough position, but is it really worth it to tell his dedicated wife, now that he is gone? To be honest, had you not seen the fleeting glance I gave Collins the other night, we wouldn't even be having this conversation," Sanchez responded.

"It's true brother. I feel the same. It would be one thing if Samuel was still alive, you may feel obligated to share this information with Maggie. But, it would do her heart no good at this point. And from where I'm sitting, it sure seems like she's been through enough," Collins voiced.

Flynn stood up, wrapped up his half eaten granola bar and he shoved it into his coat pocket.

"Let's keep moving. I'm starting to get cold."

Flynn took the lead and started traipsing through the snow at a quicker pace than before, his focus heavily on the trail in front of him.

After what had seemed like only moments to Flynn, Rose yawned and sat up, looking at her cell phone.

"Oh gosh, I didn't think I would sleep a whole hour. No wonder I need a bathroom break. Babe, can you pull into a coffee shop or gas station when you see an exit?" Rose asked.

"Yes, I can do that Rosebud. I could use a bottle of water too." Flynn replied.

Pulling up to a Kwik Trip, Flynn made a decision that he was going to let the conversation he had had with Collins and Sanchez regarding Samuel stay on the snow filled trails miles behind them. It would just do no good sharing the information with Maggie.

The guys had been right, no good would come of it.

CHAPTER 30

The day Flynn and Rose returned home, all guests had checked out and no one was scheduled to stay until Wednesday evening, so they had some private and sweet time with their babies in the quiet of their home. Though Rose loved having her Inn and living out her dream, sometimes it was a pleasant surprise to be able to live in their home as if it were just the four of them.

Flynn laid a large puffy comforter on the floor in the living room next to the warmth of the fire and he and Rose planned to have their dinner picnic-style while the girls rolled around and played. Flynn sat crossed legged between Jade and Sophia, tickling their little bellies and tenderly asking them about the fun they had over the weekend. He hadn't realized how much he too had missed their sweet, perfect little faces. Evidently he had been trying so hard to be strong for Rose, that he had fooled himself too. How lucky he was to have Rose and these two angelic twins under their roof. His wonderfully beautiful little family.

"Hon, can you take this tray? I'm going to go grab our drinks and some napkins." Rose asked, handing him a large wooden tray.

As usual his wife couldn't just make them pizza rolls and plop down next to him with a cold beer. She even made their living room picnic *Simpler Times* guest worthy.

On the tray were two small ceramic bowls filled with what Flynn guessed was potato soup. On top of the soup Rose had sprinkled a generous amount of shredded cheddar cheese and sliced green onion. In a small basket between the bowls were toasted baguette slices. She knew how much Flynn loved dipping. He smiled. *She never misses anything* he thought.

"Ok, sweetheart—here we are. Two very fancy wine glasses filled with ice water. Cheers!" Rose giggled as she handed her husband one of the crystal glasses she was holding.

"Wonderful! I needed a break from wine after this weekend, anyway. But you must have really enjoyed it, being a wine lover, huh Rose?"

"It was fun! I was delighted with all the different types we were able to sample. I didn't think your buddies would have such palettes for good wine," Rose commented while taking a seat on the blanket next to Flynn.

"Why not? You've seen too many movies about soldiers. We don't just slam shots of whiskey and arm wrestle, Rosebud!" Flynn laughed as he dunked a slice of bread in the hot soup and took a bite. "Oh, whoa—this is soooo good. I hadn't realized how hungry I was!"

Rose picked up her bowl and spooned a small taste of the soup into her mouth also.

"Mmmm, you're right—I *am* still a good cook," she said, winking. "I know babe. I wasn't generalizing you and your Army friends into a Paramount pictures production. Let's just say, I felt really very welcome with your friends and their wives and the conversation and laughs were so natural. I felt like I had known the group in another life. I can see why you are very close with them."

"That means a lot to me, Rosebud. They are like family to me."

Flynn and Rose sat and ate their meal while their baby girls were content to play with their few toys while from time to time becoming completely entranced with the flames flickering in the fireplace.

After Flynn and Rose had finished their soup and stacked the dishes back on the tray they leaned back against the couch and held each other close.

"This is *the* life, isn't it Rose? I don't say it enough, but thank you for being my wife."

Rose laid her head comfortably into the curve of Flynn's neck and closed her eyes, silently agreeing with every word he had said.

CHAPTER 31

Maggie looked at the wall calendar hanging just above the small desk in her bedroom. It was already December 16th and she had several things to do yet to be comfortably prepared for Christmas. She had to get the guest room ready for her mother who would be staying for a few days. She didn't give many gifts out, but the few she did had to be extra special and her shopping list was getting long. There were favorite cookies to make- thumbprints, Russian tea cakes and ginger snaps as well as potica and Julekake. She would wait for mom to arrive to make the potica—it was their tradition.

Smiling to herself, she grabbed the pile of mail she had been stacking over the last few days on the corner of the desk. She opened a Christmas card from Clem, one from Rose and Flynn which included a sweet photo of Jade and Sophia in their furry white bonnets and red pajamas and a sweet letter from her cousin who lived in Florida with updates on how her family was fairing. Maggie flipped through three bills—auto insurance, garbage and the wireless internet.

"Don't they know I have Christmas presents to buy? December should be no bills month," she laughed to herself as she kept sorting through a few more unopened envelopes.

Coming to a manila envelope that was unmarked, but in some way looked official, her heart began to race. Samuel was already gone and all affairs long ago handled. It couldn't be anything having to do with that. Though Maggie couldn't shake the uneasy feeling as she held it in her hands—waiting to be opened. For several minutes she stared down at the envelope wondering what could possibly be inside. Finally, realizing she'd feel better doing this with a friend close by, she grabbed her cell phone to call Rose.

After five rings, she finally picked up.

"Hello?"

"Hi Rose, I know it's a little late and you are probably exhausted from the day, but wondering if I could pop over for a short visit? Is Flynn there too?"

"Is everything all right Maggie?" Rose asked, concerned with the urgency in Maggie's voice.

"Yes, yes. At least I think so. I have a piece of mail here that is unmarked, but I can't shake the feeling that it is something regarding Samuel. Perhaps I have seen similar envelopes come while Samuel was in the military. Heaven knows he served for many years. I don't recall. But I was wondering if it might be ok to come and open it with you and Flynn present? He may even know what kind of contents could be inside before even cutting the seam. I won't stay long." Maggie promised.

"Oh, Maggie, you are always welcome here. And actually it's good timing, we just put the girls down for the night."

"Ok. Thank you Rose. I will be over in ten minutes."

On the drive to *Simpler Times*, Maggie could feel the envelope sitting in the passenger's seat like it was a red hot flame, like it was a hungry wolf staring her down—like an aggravating splinter in her skin. She just wanted it to go away.

Chances are it is nothing at all, she thought.

CHAPTER 32

TWO YEARS PRIOR

"Sergeant Ollweyes? You're being asked for by Captain Stanley in his office. He said it is urgent."

"Yes, Dawson. Please let him know I will report directly. Thank you." Samuel replied. He kept his composure at all times, especially when in the presence of rookies, such as Private Dawson who had just delivered his requested attendance. Keeping his calm was necessary and would serve his soldiers and ultimately his country the best. But, he anticipated this meeting; he didn't want to know what the next steps were going to be. Captain Stanley had been sitting on these orders for weeks. Samuel knew it would be coming.

Tucking his camouflage trousers into his boots and lacing them up tight, he grabbed his cap off a hook on the wall and left his humble room along with Maggie's loving words on notebook paper still fanned out on his bed.

When he stepped outside, the intense heat hit him like the grip of an electric fence. Jolting him into awareness. Samuel had been in Afghanistan already for ten months and he knew he wouldn't be going home at the twelve month mark. He was among the ranks that stayed until, well, he was hoping the fifteen month maximum deployment would be the reason he was leaving and not the alternative. He had made friends with many soldiers, both within his platoon and extended deep into the whole battalion. His squad, though, which consisted of seven soldiers, was as close as brotherhood. It pained him to know it was only a matter of time before they would be ordered into combat, he, then being the one giving orders. One thing he knew he would always tell a soldier's family, if he had to deliver the news of their death after they had been serving under his direction, was that he had done everything in his power to put himself in danger before their son, or daughter, husband or wife. He would gladly die ten times over than to lose one of his team. That he knew whole heartedly.

Even his forever love, Maggie, knew this truth.

Samuel's mind wandered for a few minutes while he walked through the barracks, not in as much of a hurry to see Captain Stanley as Captain Stanley thought he should be. His mind wanted to give a few short moments to thoughts of his wife back home in Minnesota.

He wondered what she would be doing at that very moment. Christmas would soon be approaching and Maggie loved the holidays. She would be hanging strings of sparkling white lights around the window frames of her shop, *The Maple Leaf*, while snowflakes fell to the ground outside. The owners of the bakery next door, Mabel and Henry Pumpernickel, would pop over for a visit with something delicious wrapped up in cellophane. Samuel could smell the frosty cold air and the hint of the sweet rolls Mabel had pulled from the oven as she presented a plateful to Maggie. Cars would be inching down the short Main Street that was Crosby, MN, some pulling into Nora's shop, *Cream and Sugar*, for a peppermint latte and a few turning down toward Clem's for a few grocery items. School buses filled with carefree kids followed behind UPS vans delivering Christmas gifts in Amazon boxes by the dozen to the doorsteps of homes down every block. Most police cars in view weren't racing after a runaway vehicle, but slowly patrolling the neighborhoods, keeping things pleasant and safe. A far cry from the city Samuel was living in currently.

He yearned for home.

But Maggie. Missing his home and the town that mimicked the simplicity of Mayberry, wasn't even worth mentioning or acknowledging without her.

She *was* his home. He happily would live right here in this dust bowl of Afghanistan for the rest of his life, if only to have her here to hold.

Samuel thought he recognized the building to his left as if he had already walked down this walkway, but he couldn't keep his foggy thoughts from picturing his beautiful wife. Maggie had the shiniest hair he had ever seen. Dark brown like melted chocolate. He loved weaving his fingers through it even if they were just sitting on the couch watching TV. Her eyes matched the warm brown of her hair. And when she looked at him with any hint of sadness, it was like looking at a little puppy dog. He would drop to his knees and give her the whole world if it was his to give. She loved life, loved her shop, her town, Samuel…But she sure deserved the baby in her arms that she so ached for. Samuel felt a pang of guilt for not being able to give her that. She would be the best mother any child could ever dream of having. He had always tried to rest on the thought that God had a different plan for him and Maggie. Only time would reveal this.

Samuel shook the thought from his head to avoid the moisture that formed in his eyes. Pulling his cap down firmly, he stood with his shoulders back and turned the doorknob to Captain Stanley's office.

CHAPTER 33

"**A**hhhh, Sergeant Ollweyes—please come in. I have the feeling you aren't at all surprised by my calling you here today?" Captain Stanley commented while standing up from his desk made of scrap plywood and dented metal pipes, a far cry from the mahogany turn of the century desk he sat at back at Fort Jefferson.

"Please, take a seat. We need to discuss some things," he offered, while gesturing to the wooden stool behind Samuel.

Samuel backed up and slowly lowered himself onto the stool, waiting for the details to come next.

Captain Stanley walked over to the small cloudy window behind his desk and looked out at the wreckage that he and Samuel had seen so many times throughout their deployments in Afghanistan that neither were all that scarred by it anymore. Still, with his back turned, the Captain began talking.

"You and I have served here more times and over more months than we care to remember, Ollweyes. I have to give you some orders that won't be easy, but are necessary and without compromise. You will most likely lose a soldier or two, or perhaps your own life, but Sergeant, we both know what we signed up for years ago."

Samuel watched Captain Stanley and saw him as he hadn't ever before. Even as clean cut, confident and posed as he always portrayed himself, he finally looked just exhausted and aged. He had been a fixture in the US Army for far longer than Samuel. He knew nothing else really, but Samuel found it strange he had never realized how worn out his Captain looked until this meeting, and this very moment.

Almost sensing that the Captain could feel his observation, Samuel replied.

"Yes, sir—we did. And, well, I'm still sure of the oath I made on day one."

"I too, Ollweyes. But, we have to accept that what we are asked to do, sometimes goes against what our conscience tells us is right. Orders do not need to be understood, they just need to be followed."

Samuel felt a sudden guilt, in which he didn't feel he earned.

"Ahh, Sir, if I may—have I gone against yours or any other commanding officer's orders?"

Captain Stanley thumped down on his chair and rubbed his forehead with his right hand.

"No, no, certainly not Sergeant. In the past, I have prided myself on coming up with the right words to say. However, I am, well, tired. I feel I can be frank with you, as we have put in the years together in serving our country. But, damn, it is getting tough."

"I understand, Captain. I do. But, really—tell me what I need to do. I can see that the mission isn't going to be an easy one. And I will do it just the same, without hesitation." Samuel spoke confidently.

"Ok, read it over, memorize it, and report back at 0600 Monday morning," Captain Stanley ordered firmly, business like again, and handed Samuel a folder. "You are free to go."

Standing, Samuel reached out and grabbed the folder. Tucking it under his left arm, he saluted the Captain with his right, and exited the office.

This time, walking at a steady pace and without an ounce of fog in his brain, he focused on getting directly back to his room and studying over the contents of the top secret file in his grasp.

CHAPTER 34

The sudden puff of gritty sand was overwhelming. Maggie coughed so hard she heaved, though her mouth and throat were void of moisture and not even saliva wet her cracked lips. Her eyes were physically scratched from debris and burned painfully. The wet, sticky feeling of the shirt fabric on her rib cage was uncomfortable, but when she tried to pull it away an excruciating pain followed. She grabbed her side and her legs gave out from under her without warning. Falling to the ground, her face hit something the size of a computer mouse, she thought, or a coin purse. The pain was so debilitating at her side, that her body wretched, this time producing bile and strings of mucus. She laid against the small object, not caring what it was. It became a stress ball of sorts, something tangible she could grasp, something she could focus on, squeeze, bite if need be.

Holding it finally in the palm of her hand she could feel the leather sole, the two small clasps on the opposite side and her fingers smeared against the same liquid that was oozing from her side. A small shoe. A tiny shoe no larger than the size of her palm. A child's shoe. What was a little girl or boy's shoe doing in this rubble. In this war ridden hell? Oh my God. Where was she? Please, please, get me out of here! She rolled back on a bed of sharp rocks and coarse sand and in the sky above her she saw flames and falling structures. As if she was underwater, she could vaguely hear the muffled sound of gunshots, explosions and terrified cries.

This cannot be real. I am dreaming. Please, I must be dreaming. Maggie thought, hoped.

Waking up with her head on a down pillow soaked in sweat and tears, Maggie struggled to catch her breath. After several moments of trying to convince herself it was only a dream, Maggie sat up on the side of her bed and focused on breathing in and out in ten second increments like her therapist had taught her.

"In………..out……..in ……..out. It was a nightmare. It is ok. You are ok."

She focused on the exercise for as long as it took for her heart to start beating at a normal, rhythmic pace. Maggie grabbed her glass of water from her night stand and took a sip. Setting it back down, she took the hair band next to it and threw her unruly hair into a messy bun. Walking over to her large twelve paned bedroom window that looked out over her serene yard, Maggie felt relief. She didn't understand what brought on the hellish nightmare, and it wasn't the first time. They were very frequent, almost a nightly routine, right after Samuel's death. But, now? At Christmas time? Over a year since his death? After she had started seeing another man?

Surely, she wasn't feeling guilty for seeing Stuart, was she? It could hardly be called a relationship. Though, she felt that was where it was headed. And truthfully, she really was starting to have feelings for him. Even the faint feeling of "butterflies" swirled around in her stomach when she saw him smile or walk toward her down the sidewalk. She had started to accept that Samuel would have been happy for her and would have wanted her to find someone. And she knew he thought Stuart was a good guy. Samuel didn't converse with him more than the semi-annual dental visits but even so, he always spoke highly of Stuart.

The return of these dreams may have something to do with the letter she had received two days prior. She had asked Flynn to sit and read it to her. It was an official document directly from The Pentagon. She had seen the return address with the official stamp: Office of the Secretary of the Army 101 Army Pentagon Washington DC. The enclosed letter itself, though printed on thick, pressed stationery, was devoid of empathy and very "to the point". It had turned Maggie off immediately, but it seemed there was some unfinished business, or unclaimed property, concerning her husband. The letter finished with the urging of an immediate response to the matter.

There were multiple ways to get in touch on the second page of the letter, but Maggie felt drained having just mustered the courage to read (or listen to) the letter. She thought she had finally let Samuel go. She would always, forever, love him. But she wanted to put this part of her life behind her. Let it rest now, peacefully. Let herself rest peacefully at night.

Evidently, this unfinished business wasn't going to allow her the respite. Her breath began quickening again, but before the only option to settle down was to breathe into a brown paper bag, she pounded her fist on the windowsill, deciding she'd had enough for today.

Maggie opted on a refreshing shower that might help clear her head and wash away any lasting tremors from the dream. She walked into the bathroom attached to her bedroom and flipped the warm water on, steam filling the room. She undressed and stepped under the shower head turning it to the massage setting. The hard, pelting drops of water felt good against her back and shoulders. She leaned forward and let it beat down until her skin was red. She squirted some jasmine vanilla shampoo in the palm of her hand and lathered her hair until it was frothy with soap suds. She followed with a smooth conditioner and after rinsing, turned off the running water.

Maggie dried off and wrapped herself like a burrito in an oversized, puffy white bath towel. She felt better. Refreshed, rejuvenated and pretty much ready to tackle the day like any other. If she had learned anything from living through tragedy, it was that there was no choice than to pick yourself up and move on.

CHAPTER 35

TWO YEARS PRIOR

S amuel sat in the back of the covered Army truck with his team, in full combat gear and armed with attack weaponry. His stomach threatened to regurgitate the bland breakfast of dry wheat toast and half a cup of milk he had forced down hours ago. It wasn't that he was ill prepared for his mission. He had studied the contents of the folder Captain Stanley had given him a week ago until it was imprinted in his brain like the urge to breathe or swallow. Likewise, his team was well prepped for the mission at hand.

Even without seeing outside the canvas draped truck, he knew they were not far from their target. He took only a last five second glance up at the faces of his seven teammates, hoping and praying they would all be spared from the dangers of death they would surely face soon.

God, please watch over my boys. If someone should be sacrificed today, please let it be me. I, like you did, would gladly lay down my own life for theirs. They are innocent humans with families, children, loved ones and I just can't bear the thought of seeing them perish in this place. ... Thy will be done. Amen.

It all happened very fast. Samuel hopped out of the truck, quietly instructing Thompson, then Garcia, Kostavich, Williams, Tilman, Kwan and lastly Sheffield to exit and stand still. They hid behind a dilapidated auto repair shop that was just yards from their targeted building, a Taliban meeting house. The main point, the whole mission in the US military being over here was to rid the country of this evil force.

Today, they would do their part in accomplishing that.

CHAPTER 36

Rose spread a generous amount of butter over the rectangle slab of sweet roll dough and followed with the cinnamon sugar mixer. Very carefully she started rolling the dough tight, sealing the end by pinching the dough together at the seam. As she snipped a long strand of twine to cut the dough into rolls, she remembered events from the night before. Maggie had received a letter, an important letter, directly from The Pentagon. She had been nervous to open it and read the words without a friend at her side. Even though she realized she had already suffered the immense pain of losing her husband, there was just something that caused extreme anxiety when receiving an envelope such as this one, a year later.

Of course Rose and Flynn asked her to come right over and they would be happy to be with her. She was glad when Flynn went so far as to offer to read it to Maggie. She seemed momentarily embarrassed, but relieved and handed over the envelope for Flynn to open and read the contents inside.

After lining the pinwheel rolls in neat rows in her pan, Rose covered it with a thin kitchen towel, leaving them to rise. Wiping her hands on her apron, she walked over to the sink to wash her prep bowls. The squeak of the kitchen door surprised her.

"Good morning Rosebud. You sure were up early this morning. I guess it must be cinnamon roll day huh?" Flynn guessed, while he leaned down and kissed Rose on the cheek.

"Yes, that's right. She answered simply, while scrubbing the glass bowl in her hands and rinsing.

"What is it, Rose? You seem troubled or distracted. Is something wrong?" Flynn asked.

"I don't know. I just was thinking back to last night with Maggie and the letter you read to her. She seemed to just want to bury it and pretend it had never been delivered. Not that I blame her. She's been through hell and back this last year. But, it has to be something extremely important the letter referred to, or it would not be urging her immediate attention. And I got the feeling she may just brush it off." Rose turned and looked up at her husband's face. "Am I imagining it, Flynn?"

Flynn reached up and dusted a streak of flour from his wife's cheek with his thumb and held her face in his hands.

"No, you aren't imagining it. But, I've seen reactions like this before. She is scared. She knows her husband is gone, but the thought of digging up the past, most especially when it involves Samuel's death, is something she can't bring herself to process right now."

Rose fiddled with the hem of Flynn's jacket, nervously.

"But, this is something she can't leave undone. It is imperative that she responds. Right?"

"She will."

Rose noticed a last look of sympathy in his eyes before he kissed her goodbye and left for work.

She watched out the kitchen window until the tail lights of Flynn's truck were out of sight. She thought of what her dear friend was going through, what she had gone through, and realized it could be her in the same situation.

Flynn, what would I do without you.

CHAPTER 37

Maggie sat on a leather, high back armchair in her store, leisurely sipping on a cup of coffee – relaxing instead of working, for a change. Muffin sat cuddled between the side of the chair and Maggie's leg and was purring loudly as she scratched the cat's head. Watching the dark winter morning slowly turn into a bustling world outside her front window, Maggie decided she had better start her day.

The shop had been quite busy as the days leading up to Christmas dwindled. Restocking ornaments, slippers, pajamas, blankets, and cookie baking kits was on the agenda for today. Maggie, even a few days later, still felt a tad perturbed by the letter she had received. Something kept her from acknowledging its existence in her desk drawer, but something else kept her from throwing it out in the trash can.

"Ugh, Muffin. I don't know what to do."

She set her warm mug down on a table nearby and picked up her cuddly cat. She needed a close snuggle from a friend, even if it meant from a furry feline. As if sensing what Maggie needed, Muffin nuzzled under Maggie's chin and they sat in a cozy embrace until the sun had finally risen into the morning sky. Clouds had parted and the rays made the snow shimmer with an almost blinding glare.

Before Maggie could get the gumption to stand up and start her day, the bells on her front door jingled.

Well, good morning Maggie. I don't think I've ever noticed your cat here in the shop. I see she's a snuggler huh?" Stuart commented with a smile.

Maggie laughed and set Muffin down in a basket of blankets where she gladly curled up to finish her nap.

"Yes, she is that. I'm glad I decided to adopt her as a shop companion. She does very good work here for me."

"Oh, I'm sure. It looks like she is just full of energy today." he teased.

Maggie retrieved her mug and walked toward the back counter.

"So, what are you up to today, Stuart?"

Following Maggie, Stuart piped up.

"Well, as a matter of fact, I was wondering if you would come with me this evening to listen to some live music at the brewery? We could sip on a couple beers and share a pizza if you are up to it?" he asked, hopeful.

Maggie wanted to. She even felt the butterflies again as he asked. But, something felt strange now that the letter had ended up in her hands. Her mind was all jumbled up and she didn't know what to do or how to deal with it.

She started folding holiday baby blankets and stacking them in wicker baskets to set out in the display window. After several silent seconds, she could feel Stuart's unease.

"Is that a no, Maggie? You know I never want to be pushy. It's really only a friendly night out. I am satisfied to only be your friend if that's what you want."

"Stuart. Umm. It's not that I don't want to go. It sounds like fun. Really, it does. I, well, tonight just won't work. But, maybe another night?" Maggie formed the words, but it sure felt unnatural to say them out loud to him.

"Of course Maggie. Anytime." Stuart reached down petting Muffin for a brief minute. "Have a good day, Muffin."

He waved to Maggie before walking out the front door.

"Damn it." Maggie whispered to herself.

CHAPTER 38

TWO YEARS PRIOR

"Ok, wait for my go-ahead." Samuel ordered his team before their carefully constructed plan of attack became operational. One last glance at his team of loyal and proud men, looking ready and full of adrenaline, he edged forward with his back to the stone wall, motioning with his left hand to follow. All eight of the soldiers edged cautiously, firearms up, aimed and ready, eyes moving left and right, up and down, feet sliding inch by inch behind the soldier in front of them. They moved as a solid unit, each sensing what the other was feeling, a tiny misstep or unusual movement causing concern of enemy presence. All the while doing it with beads of sweat running down their cheeks and necks under heavy helmets in 100 degrees plus temperatures.

After what had felt like several minutes of waiting in terrifying anticipation, Samuel gave the silent order using hand gestures only. His team knew they would filter into the front entrance of the building and proceed through each room, inspecting every inch for signs that the Taliban had occupied the premises. At this point, all they needed was to see his arm raised and they knew what to do next.

Still holding their firearms upright and aimed, the soldiers strategically slipped through the front door and breaking into groups, went from room to room, as per mission instruction. Samuel had Williams and Kwan at his back. They were all focused and ready for the tiniest hint of movement. Samuel could faintly hear Williams breathing heavily right behind him. Private Williams was the youngest among the group at only twenty-three years of age. He was an exceptionally smart, sharp and agile kid who aimed to please his commanding officers. But, with the very little experience he'd had in actual combat, Samuel was especially concerned with his composure on this mission. In fact it was the very reason he had placed Williams directly between him and Kwan.

Samuel kept tight against the dark wall, feeling the crumbling of plaster behind his back crunch with each slight movement. He crisscrossed each stride attempting the lightest of steps, pretending he was wearing his sheepskin slippers rather than heavy steel toed combat boots.

Finally making it down the dusty hallway to the first room on the right he stopped and raised his M4 rifle and swiftly stepped through the open door frame. Before he knew what was happening there were clouds of dust and commotion and some kind of screeching. He couldn't see, he didn't know what was coming at him, but he crouched to one knee, rifle still aimed. After a few seconds, he realized he was being assaulted by a thick flock of pigeons who had been roosting in this abandoned building. Though his heart was beating out of his chest Samuel almost laughed when the birds finally found an escape through the 6 ft hole in the roof above. Even though he had heard flocks of pigeons were not uncommon in the Kabul area, sometimes hundreds roosting together in large abandoned buildings such as this, he was not prepared for such an attack.

Shaking it off, Samuel turned back to Williams and Kwan giving them a thumbs up. Again, Samuel could tell that the sudden excitement had only intensified Williams's anxiety. He had to do something. Wrapping his left hand around the back of Williams's neck, Samuel pulled him closer.

"Listen Private, you have to remember that I chose you to be at my side on this mission. I trust you, your team trusts you, and I wouldn't have brought you if I wasn't 100% sure you were ready. Look at me Williams."

Williams finally turned his attention to Samuel and looked him in the eyes.

"Breathe in for ten seconds, hold it for ten and breathe out for ten."

Williams began to shake his head and look around as if the enemy lurked.

"No, don't look over there or over there either. Look at me and do as I say. We have time. You must, soldier. We need you today. Now breathe in, hold it and breathe out like I instructed and then believe and trust in your abilities."

Samuel watched as Williams did just that. He did the same and glanced at Kwan, who appeared to be indulging in a quick breather himself.

Half the training for combat was the actual tactical teaching and the other half-practicing the art of collectedness. At least this was Samuel's belief. Expertly trained or not, if a soldier loses his cool during combat, the training no longer can serve him well.

Samuel saw a new confidence in Williams's face. Was he scared? Hell yea, who wasn't? But, he had found control and was now ready to continue on, wherever *on* was.

CHAPTER 39

Maggie enjoyed snowshoeing. It was an activity she and Samuel would do on pleasant winter days on the beautiful trails in the Cuyuna area where they lived. In truth she hadn't been super excited to get into it, but Samuel, a man she knew couldn't sit still, loved trying new things. And so he had purchased two pairs for he and Maggie. He promised they wouldn't go on days that the temperatures reached below zero and even then they could keep close.

But what he didn't know is that after his death, on winter days, she had loved traipsing through the snow. The cool, exhilarating air was intoxicating. The rhythmic paces of her feet moving miles through snowy terrain felt like an accomplishment every time. Mostly though, when she reached the part of the trail, a half a mile away from town, where things still looked almost untouched, she found serenity. The tall white pines stood confidently and protectively over the ice covered mine pits deep beneath the banks of frozen iron ore dusted generously with a blanket of snow.

Maggie huffed and puffed and with every breath in and out she gained focus and a new determination she had been longing for. A determination to face this aggravating letter she received from The Pentagon. Yes, the actual United States of America Pentagon. She had been hoping the manila envelope would vanish into thin air, and that her realization of it being a dream would come to pass. But after days… she had accepted it as a reality.

It had to be dealt with.

Picking up the pace Maggie yearned to feel exertion like she hadn't felt for years. When she saw a hill in the distance, she charged it. When she felt beads of sweat wetting her eyebrow, she pushed harder. Pulling off her long, down coat, she tied it haphazardly around her waist and continued at a ridiculous pace. It felt good to be consumed by something other than the constant thought of her husband's death, the pain and agony and days of numbness following. But this new focus, clawing at her attention, was the letter. It wasn't going away. She knew this and had to reply.

The other question, obviously so, was what more do they want? Why, after months and months had gone by, why did they have to reach out to her regarding some random personal effects that were recovered? Samuel was gone from her life, with all due respect – six feet under. She had buried her feelings with him a long time ago. She assumed it was protocol, however, it still seemed inhumane.

For God's sake, let me move on.

Maggie came up the hill to an overlook with Pennington Mine Pit as the picturesque display below. Even frozen over it was a breathtaking sight. She could see for miles every way she turned. With the adrenaline in her veins still pulsing and her breathing taking its time to slow, she couldn't keep the flood of emotion from erupting. Finding a stump close by, she allowed herself a rest and with that a few tears.

"Maggie, what did I tell ya? I told you that you'd eventually see the joy in snow shoeing didn't I? And here you are making it all the way out to Pennington in half the time we used to do it together. Oh, no – don't cry harder because I said *together*. Please my love, I could never bear to see you in pain. The truth is, I'm glad you are out here alone with your thoughts. I hope that you can find it in yourself to gather the courage to reply to the recent letter you have received. It is…Well I had hoped it wouldn't have taken so very long to get to you. But, there is nothing that can be done about that. All that can be done is to acknowledge it has come, and that it is awaiting your reply. Maggie, I do encourage you to move on and find happiness. In fact, I couldn't have chosen a better second to me, than Dr. Vontrapp. What a solid, good guy. I mean it. I wish I didn't have to fade like the snow flurries swirling over the treetops. Be well my love, my wife, be well."

Maggie felt the words as if Samuel had been sitting next to her whispering them into her ear.

She also felt there was nothing more to do than to turn around and make the trip back home.

CHAPTER 40

TWO YEARS PRIOR

S amuel, Kwan and Williams continued through the dusty and increasingly dark and tight hallways. Not one to dramatize anything, Samuel kept pushing away the ominous feeling that crept into his veins with each step he took toward the back of the dwelling. Something wasn't sitting right. Should he trust his gut or keep a sane, steady head as an experienced officer was taught to?

For a moment he saw what was in front of him. An abandoned building, how old, he wasn't sure. It was crumbling, regardless.

Soldiers that were sent to war were taught actual exercises in blocking out foul smells as it was a common inconvenience. Until that moment, Samuel hadn't noticed the putrid smell of excrement lurking, the musty scent of black mold and decades of grime that lay beneath his feet and up against his back. Why were these insignificant details seeping into his senses at such a perilous time. Suddenly he noticed a ripped tapestry hanging on a nail by only frayed threads. A chipped water pitcher lay on the floor that had once filled glasses for a family to drink from. A wooden chair tipped over, a chewed up pillow spewing goose down feathers, a child's bouncy ball that disturbed him to the point of breaking. All of it wasn't natural

It hit him as it had never before and suddenly Samuel realized he wanted to go home. After this mission, which he promised to give his all to, he was going to turn in his papers for the request of retirement. It may be two years at most, but at that exact moment, though a strange place for such clarity, he had made up his mind.

He wanted more time with the only thing that truly mattered to him... Maggie.

CHAPTER 41

"**C**an you repeat your name ma'am? Was it Maggie Ollweyes? Sergeant Samuel Ollweyes's wife?"

"Yes, that is correct. I received a letter coming directly from the office of the Secretary of the Army. As far as informative content, there really wasn't any, except the request of my immediate response."

"I see Mrs. Ollweyes. May I place you on hold while I transfer you to Captain Stanley's office?"

"I'm looking at the letter here. It doesn't say that it came from Captain Stanley, directly." Maggie replied, a large knot forming in her chest at the mention of Samuel's commanding officer.

"No. That is because he may not have written the letter directly, but he certainly would have given the direction to do so. As you said, the letter was rather vague, but to the point, and signed by no one," the lady on the other end of the phone retorted. "Nothing is done by the US military halfway or in an incomplete manner, Mrs. Ollweyes, with all due respect. So, again, I will ask that you hold while I transfer you to Captain Stanley's office. And before you become anxious about speaking to the Captain, don't, because it will be one of his secretaries or officers that will initially take the call."

"I see. Then, by all means, please place me on hold." Maggie was beginning to wonder if she had made the right decision. So much red tape it seemed. Captain Stanley was Samuel's commanding officer, but she knew how much Samuel respected the man, looked up to him and they were friends too. This isn't just regular Army procedure. If Benjamin Stanley was giving the initial direction to get in touch with Maggie, it was coming from a place that was important. Perhaps important to Samuel before his death.

But what? And why now? Maggie wondered what in the world could be so pressing. Samuel was gone. She had seen his lifeless body, held his cold hand, cried while she closed his heavy oak casket and watched as it was lowered into the ground. She remembered tossing a large bouquet of irises into the hole immediately after, her mind not grasping the finality of what was playing out in front of her.

As Maggie sat for several more minutes on hold, her mind wandered. She felt a feather light breeze on her cheek, the morning sun creeping up over the hillside just ahead on the trail. Though fuzzy, she could see an image coming closer. She could barely make out if the image was anything more than a mixture of watercolors before it materialized into a person right in front of her. The warmth in his smile and the purity in his blue eyes proved who it was. Imagined or not, it was her Samuel.

"Maggie, come with me. This is something you will want to see!" Samuel told her excitedly.

She gladly took his hand in hers and followed. He had led her down hills and up, through trails weaving between thick poplar overgrowth and wide open alfalfa fields. Finally, about the time Maggie was going to ask when they were getting to their destination, Samuel pushed through the cover of two large pine branches and into a sea of purple that Maggie thought looked like an image of heaven. Deep hues of purple, lavender and violet swayed in the light air. The unique blooms making their presence known immediately.

"Samuel, what is this? It is breathtaking. I have never in my wildest dreams seen so many irises. It is, well, simply beautiful." She brought her hands to her heart as she took the sight in.

"Come, sit."

He softly guided her to a plush blanket he had laid out in the midst of the massive garden.

After they had enjoyed a picnic of crackers, cheddar cheese slices, black berries and almonds, they made love while the flowers surrounding them continued to sway in the light breeze. Lounging on the blanket, staring at the clouds above, Samuel had told Maggie that irises were symbols of hope and faith. He had leaned over her, focusing seriously into her eyes, telling her that he was certain she would be a mother someday. Maggie had cried at his certainty. After so many years of trying, it had seemed hopeless. But, Samuel, at that moment, knew.

Though the memory of that day beneath tall purple irises brought her a deep longing for Samuel's touch, Maggie still couldn't forgive him for dying.

CHAPTER 42

Rose carefully transferred the whipped shortbread cookies, each topped with a fancy maraschino cherry, onto a simple paper plate and covered it with plastic wrap. "Lucille? Marie?" She called up the stairs. "I am off to my dental appointment."

"Ok, Rosie. No problem. We are a-ok here with the babies." Marie replied, peeking over the banister.

Rose didn't love going to the dentist. It was something she put off and rescheduled appointments for no good reason. But, it had been almost a year since her last exam and it was time.

Having been somewhat of a friend with Dr. Vontrapp since he and Maggie had become closely acquainted, she thought it a nice gesture to bring him and his staff a plate of her favorite whipped shortbread cookies. It was only five or six blocks away and the weather was rather mild, so Rose decided to walk.

During her walk she thought about Maggie and contemplated stopping into her shop. Rose wanted to ask if she had responded yet to the letter. But, even a week later, she hadn't decided whether it was her place to pry. They had become so close and yet Rose hadn't heard a peep from Maggie since the night Flynn had read her the letter word for word in their living room.

Clem was wiping down a window and she waved. She smiled as Mrs. Chisholm shuffled past on the sidewalk with her sweater clad Corgi. It was a rare occasion that Rose ventured out into the hubbub that was Main Street mornings. She enjoyed it for a change of pace. Though, she had to admit, nothing topped stoking a fire and setting out fresh coffee and scones at *Simpler Times* at sunrise.

Rose kicked her boots lightly against the last step and pulled open the door of Dr. Vontrapp's dental clinic. As always the smell of minty toothpaste, rubbing alcohol and bleach seeped into her nostrils giving her a good dose of anxiety.

"Rose! Hi. You are right on time, my dear," Lydia greeted from behind the reception desk.

"Hi Lydia. How are you?" Rose replied.

"Doing great. How are things down at *Simpler Times*? Keeping a full house?"

"We are. Though I suspect a lull maybe after the holidays? Who knows. But, for now, I am very grateful," Rose replied. "Should I take a seat?"

"Yes, go ahead. Though I think Stuart will be ready for you shortly."

"Thank you. Oh, I almost forgot. These are for you, well you and the staff," Rose said, handing the plate of cookies to Lydia.

"Awwww, how thoughtful of you. They look too beautiful to eat!" Lydia complimented.

Rose smiled and took a seat in the waiting room across from a mother with two young children wearing frowns. No doubt they were thinking the only occasion they'd rather be at school was when they were having a dental exam. Rose had a similar sentiment, but she hid it with a cheery disposition.

"Rose? You can come on back." Jessie, one of the hygienists, called to her. After she had been led to the second exam room, and was seated and tipped back in the chair, it was only moments before Stuart popped his head around the corner.

"Mrs. Mitchell, Rose, nice to see you. How have things been going at the Inn during the holiday season? I imagine quite busy," he said, making light conversation while he rolled closer on his stool.

"Yes, in fact, all rooms are full this week. I love it though, as busy as I am. Christmas time, joyful families, a brightly lit Frasier fir in our living room for guests to sit around. The smell of cookies and candies coming from the kit—" Rose stopped herself, suddenly embarrassed for rambling like a page out of her holiday classics book. "Sorry. I guess you can see I am passionate about what I do."

Stuart laughed.

"Hey, it's wonderful. I am too. And that being said, let's lean you back and take a look at your teeth shall we?"

Like any exam, conversation was minimal in between the scraping, buzzing, spraying and spitting. But after Stuart sat Rose back up and told her all looked well, he didn't seem to make a quick effort to leave right away. Rose got the idea he wanted to ask her something. The silence started to create a touch of awkwardness and so Rose took it upon herself to speak first.

"Ahh Stuart, have you seen Maggie lately? She must be so busy at the shop. I haven't heard from her in days."

"To be honest, I was going to ask the same. I did make a quick visit to *The Maple Leaf* earlier in the week and…well, I got the feeling something was troubling her. In fact, I don't know if it's right of me to say, but it felt as if she didn't want me there at all."

Stuart stood up removing his plastic gloves and tossed them in the trash can, forcing the casual gesture.

"Hmmm, that's what I was afraid of. Don't worry, Stuart. This has nothing to do with you. Maggie has some heavy stuff on her plate right now. But I can see I need to check in on her. Please, just give her a little space. I promise she will come around once she figures out how to deal with some challenges she's been given."

"Hmmm Well, I hope it is nothing too serious." Stuart smiled, but before leaving the room, he paused again.

"Rose, would you tell her I'm here for her? I know she maybe isn't ready for dating, just yet, but either way — I can be a good listener and friend."

"I'll tell her Stuart. And thank you."

Rose felt a rush of admiration for Stuart at that moment and at the same instant, a deep concern for her friend.

A visit to *The Maple Leaf* on the walk home was going to be a must.

CHAPTER 43

TWO YEARS PRIOR

Samuel couldn't make sense of the next several minutes. There was an explosion that seemed to have come from the back of the building. He had given his troops the order to use explosive weaponry if confirmed Taliban soldiers were present as suspected. What worried him, was they had not checked all areas and couldn't possibly be sure yet that others, perhaps innocent civilians, even children, weren't also within these walls.

He, Kwan and Williams had not been seriously injured nor did any of them lay unconscious, but the impact of the detonated hand grenade sent a jolt so strong all three soldiers were knocked off their feet.

After the deafening blast and the explosion induced whiplash, Samuel, Kwan and Williams lay on their backs covered in bits of plaster gasping for air to return to their lungs. Shaking off the temporary daze, Samuel rolled to his side and tapped Kwan on the chest. He pointed his finger twice toward the door. They needed to make their way down the hall and find the source of the explosion and confirm the remaining team members were ok. Kwan shook Wiliams firmly. Finally, he found his bearings as well as his gun and followed as they continued the mission at hand.

Inching down the dark hallway, Samuel could see a slight glow coming from a flashlight. His heart jumped knowing at least some of his team was still alive, perhaps all of them. God willing.

Though all of his soldiers were alive, some had sustained injuries that required medical attention. He motioned to fall back, but no one moved.

Sheffield came to Samuel's side, looked him in the eyes and nodded for him to follow into the nearby room. Samuel knew not one soldier on his team would question his order, unless there had been a worthy reason.

Sheffield guided him until they reached the opening to a small room and stepped in. Realization hit him with more force than the impact of the explosion moments ago.

Somehow the mission had failed and he was faced with something he hadn't been given the training for.

CHAPTER 44

"**M**aggie, are you here?" Rose called as she opened the door to *The Maple Leaf,* the sleigh bells jingling cheerfully as she entered. Finding Maggie in the back room, sitting on a stool holding her cat Muffin close, was enough to bring a concerned crinkle to Rose's eyebrows. Yes Maggie loved her ball of fluff cat, but sitting in the back room among boxes and discarded bubble wrap holding her cat close in the middle of the shop's open hours seemed enough reason for Rose to intrude.

"Ahem, Maggie?" Rose cleared her throat rather loudly.

"Oh my! Rose??" Maggie responded, tossing poor Muffin in the air.

"Maggie, what are you doing back here in the storage room? You ok?" Rose asked.

"Yes, yes. Just taking a quick break. What brings you here?"

"Well, it so happens I had a dentist appointment with Dr. Vontrapp, and decided to pay you a visit afterward. It has been days since we heard from you, Maggie."

Maggie walked out of the box filled room, closing the door behind her. Realizing her holiday playlist had ended, she found the echo dot and started it over with the push of a button.

"I know, Rose. I'm sorry. I have been so busy, what with the holidays and all. Christmas time brings lots of shoppers, as you know."

Rose grabbed her friend's hand and walked her over to two wooden chairs sitting together on either side of a lovely vintage tea table.

"Maggie, can we sit a minute?"

Maggie plunked down in the chair across from Rose, looking defeated.

"Rose, yes I did call. I have a meeting on December 20th, with Officer Sheffield. Evidently he was close with Samuel during his last deployment. Captain Stanley will be present at his best effort, but may not be able to attend due to other important obligations."

Maggie rubbed her forehead with both hands, squeezing harder than Rose guessed a human head would prefer to be. She fiddled with a hand woven doily that sat beneath an ornate lamp. It was difficult to sit still or to make small talk. She felt such an anxiety in the pit of her stomach.

"Maggie, did they tell you anything about why you are being asked to come all the way to Washington DC for this meeting? Why can't it be done by teleconference or even a Zoom meeting? I realize that would be a bit more impersonal, but perhaps you'd prefer it? It's strange they didn't ask." Rose pondered.

"Well, evidently it is something very important, perhaps involving classified information that hadn't been released directly after Samuel's death? I can't begin to guess."

Rose was deep in thought, wondering if Flynn might have some speculations as to why the requested in-person meeting. She was anxious to speak with him over dinner tonight.

"Listen Maggie, everything is going to be ok. There may be some additional information that can't be released without having shared it with you in person. This is probably just protocol. In any case, you shouldn't work yourself up so terribly about it, my friend." Rose consoled her.

Maggie stood up and began rearranging a shelf of Christmas gnomes, no longer able to sit still. She knew Rose was probably right. Why was she so on edge about this? Perhaps, it was all too similar to the events of just over a year ago, when she had been informed of Samuel's death. It just all came flooding back. And just when she was finally finding herself crawling out of the dark hole she had been stuck in.

Rose zipped up her coat and wrapped her red scarf around her neck, ready for her walk back home.

Giving Maggie a light squeeze on her shoulder she smiled.

"Let me know if I can do anything for you, Maggie. You know where I'll be."

"Thank you. I will."

Maggie continued busily rearranging anything she could find in her shop to keep her hands moving and mind focused elsewhere in between groups of customers popping in from time to time.

Even with all the focus of their conversation being on her meeting regarding her late husband, it still hadn't escaped Maggie's attention when Rose had mentioned having come from Stuart's office, after her dental visit.

There was something there she couldn't deny.

She didn't think it would happen again so fast and for that she felt guilty. But, if she was being honest to herself, she could see a real future with Stuart. She could feel herself missing him, longing for him, wishing he'd stop by.

It added all kinds of confusing dimensions to the fix she was in. How could she concentrate on this new mysterious information involving Samuel, and still give deserved attention to Stuart. Even if she decided to continue the obvious road the two were on, for now, she would be far too distracted.

For a reason she couldn't rightly identify, Maggie threw the last several ornaments she had been arranging on a nearby loveseat and walked straight to where her coat and purse hung on a hook next to the back exit. Switching the lights off and locking the door- Maggie walked to her jeep.

She cranked the key revving the engine loud in the cold temps of the evening.

"I could use a drink." Maggie said out loud.

CHAPTER 45

Maggie pulled into the wine bar on 6th Street, eager to sit at a back high top table, sip on a glass of local wine and listen to the guitar music coming from tonight's scheduled musician. She may run into a few Crosby townspeople having an after work meeting over a charcuterie board, but nothing that would require more than a sweet smile and "Hi, how are you all this evening?"

Minutes ago, in the midst of her obsessive organizing of antique ornaments and hand crafted Christmas gnomes, Maggie had had enough. Enough of the actual act of setting each carefully on shelves and tree branches? She thought not. It was the consistent thoughts whirling around in her mind that she had enough of. She needed a break!

As she filled up her glass with a sparkling pink Rose' she glanced across the room at a similar high top corner table and realized her break was not going to happen tonight.

Stuart looked up from his phone the moment she had allowed her eyes to recognize it was him sitting across the room from her. Was he stalking her, or was this a total coincidence? The look on his face told her that he was as surprised as she was. Seeing there was no other way to enjoy the night alone while also avoiding the awkward glances across the room at each other, Maggie waved Stuart over to her table. She noticed as he made his way across the room, several folks stopped him to say hello or shake his hand. Being the gentleman he was, he took the time with each friend or patient as they greeted him.

"I knew that would happen," he laughed.

"You're a popular guy I guess." Maggie winked while she tipped her wine glass to her lip. *Ugh, why am I flirting with him?*

"No, no. Not popular. That I've never been. Nice? Polite? Maybe. But popular? In high school I was the small, scrawny kid who wore thick glasses and never went to prom. I guess now it's all still true, except I wear contacts."

This time he winked at Maggie.

Why is he more attractive now that I told myself I needed to put this on hold? This isn't the time! She was having a hard time concentrating on that very thought, when her eyes kept glancing at his lips as he spoke, his hands as he grasped the stem of his dark burgundy.

"I always had a soft spot for geeks," she said, before she could take back the words.

"What I mean is…you aren't one. But the way you described yourself painted the picture of a geek, or what one might describe a so-called "geek" as. Though I'm sure you weren't actually. Ugh, I give up, Stuart."

Stuart watched as Maggie's cheeks turned the color of the Rose' she was sipping on. He looked at her without laughing or smiling and made no effort to divert his eyes. He didn't know what stresses were complicating Maggie's life, he didn't care. He knew he liked her before, but this was something different. It scared him a bit.

"Ahem, so…I was looking at one of these appetizers," he said nervously, picking up the menu between them and reading each to himself. "You interested in sharing something?"

"I hadn't even thought of it just yet to be honest. But, sure, why not? You pick an item or two. I'm going to run to the ladies room."

Maggie too felt a bit flustered with the rush of feelings she had felt when Stuart had just stared into her eyes. He had a smile that made her weak in the knees, but this stare?

It unnerved her.

As she looked in the mirror and fixed a few fly away hairs, she asked the reflection, "What do I do? I feel ready. I know there is a real chemistry here. Is it ok to enjoy myself?"

Maggie dabbed on a few drops of Burberry Brit on her wrists and neck and applied a fresh layer of tinted lip balm. The act of beautifying herself for someone other than Samuel gave her a momentary stab of guilt. She frowned and almost started talking to herself again, before she heard someone coming in.

A server wearing a white dress shirt and long black apron tied around her waist walked in quickly.

"Oh my goodness! I am so sorry. I just about knocked you over by bolting in here so fast."

She looked at Maggie's stunned face for a second. "You sure you're ok?"

Maggie smiled. "Oh no harm done at all. You are very busy out there, so I can understand the hurry to fit in a bathroom break."

The two laughed. As Maggie was opening the door to leave she noticed the woman's name tag pinned to her shirt.

"Faith."

Find Faith. There was that word again. A warm feeling came upon her and she knew what she wanted to do. What she felt in her heart she could allow herself to do.

As she sat back on her stool, opposite Stuart, she felt at peace, if only for the moment.

"Should we have one more glass while we wait for the appetizers?"

CHAPTER 46

TWO YEARS PRIOR

Samuel sat in a private room in the small hospital. He waited on the attending doctor to share some vital news with him. Worry written on his face in the still sweat and dirt filled creases over his forehead and around his eyes. Traces of blood had dried on his sleeves and as he nervously bounced his left knee he noticed a large rip in his trousers. His mind reeled. Having the need to rush for medical attention, the events leading up to the explosion were still unknown. In the midst of the current situation, he would need to wait until later to learn where things went wrong.

Naturally, as commanding officer, the head of his team, senior to all of his soldiers, he felt responsible. And ultimately, he was. That was how it worked. Someone had to bear that.

This time – it was he who wore the hat.

Tilman had sustained burns on his hands and neck. Samuel had yet to learn to what degree, though with his consistent fall into and out of consciousness he feared they were serious. Garcia's lower leg had been trapped under a large beam that had fallen during the crash. Among the obvious tears and lacerations to his skin and muscle, several bones had been broken.

His soldiers were being taken care of by highly skilled surgeons as he waited. But what the doctor was coming to speak to him further about was regarding the civilians that had been in the building at the time of the explosion.

Earlier Sheffield had guided Samuel to a small room just down the hall from where the grenade had been detonated. Hiding beneath a heavy canvas drape Sheffield had located a man, woman and child. To be more precise – an infant which added to the shock. The man had taken the obvious blow from the crash and due to head injuries, Samuel guessed what he hoped to not be true. The woman was hanging on, but she too had several injuries – some internal from the information he had already heard. The baby, miraculously, having been sheltered carefully beneath her parents, had only a few bruises and a cut on her cheek.

Samuel folded his hands and rested his forehead on them. He prayed. He bargained with God. He tried to ask for help, forgiveness, anything he could do to save these innocent people. He had, of course, already done so for his team before the mission had even started. But, they knew what they had signed up for. They had all known at any moment it could be their time.

Picturing Maggie fighting for her life in the humble hospital bed just a few rooms down from where he sat now sent a shiver through him. And to think of their baby? Here? Cries left unheard. The comforts of her mama or dad no longer offered due to a mission he choreographed. He could hardly breathe for the burden of pain that was on his hands.

What could he do? Except have faith that God would show him.

CHAPTER 47

"Captain Silva? A word sir?" Flynn peeked in from behind the office door.

The captain looked up from his notes and with his left hand motioned for Flynn to take a seat opposite him from across his large, mahogany desk.

After Flynn sat down, the captain spoke.

"What can I do for you, Officer Mitchell?"

Flynn had rehearsed how he would ask this question a number of times an hour ago, but still it felt a bit meddlesome.

"Sir, umm, forgive me, but I am good friends with Sergeant Ollweyes' widow, Maggie. She has been summoned, if you will, to a meeting involving an apparent urgent matter involving her late husband. Off the record, and with all due respect, sir – do you have any idea what such a meeting could be involving?"

Flynn had really not wanted to go to his senior commander to ask such a – well – silly question, but Rose had begged. Evidently the letter Maggie had received was causing her extreme stress even though a meeting was on the calendar. Flynn, himself, had offered to go with Maggie, but she was determined to attend it herself. Perhaps she was worried about what information might be shared.

"Officer, of course you know I have no idea, nor authorization to inquire," Captain Silva expressed.

"You, of course, sir. To be honest, my wife Rose has become so close with Maggie and seen the distress she is in. Well, she basically begged me to see you." Flynn admitted honestly.

The captain's mouth turned into a very slight smile, though Flynn noticed it.

"I wish I could keep all grieving wives, well families, from continual distress, but I don't have that power. What my guess is, and I would say my guess is fairly accurate, is that this is involving some unfinished business Samuel Ollweyes had. Mitchell, if a soldier dies, is buried and the file is closed, the family doesn't hear anything further. If a soldier dies, is buried, but the file is not closed – these meetings are requested. And as you can imagine, they need to be dealt with immediately." With that Captain Silva picked up his pen and began writing in his notepad again. Flynn stood up.

"Thank you for your time, Sir."

Flynn turned on his heel and opened the door to leave.

"Mitchell? I extend my deepest sympathy to Maggie Ollweyes. And, I trust, dare I say, I have faith, all will go well with her meeting at The Pentagon."

Flynn nodded, as did Captain Sliva, and he walked out, shutting the door behind him.

CHAPTER 48

Maggie looked up at the stars that decorated the black sky, and the glare around the moon creating a perfect ring. On winter nights she noticed this more prominently. She had yet to Google the natural phenomenon, but for now her mind was on something far more important.

"Stuart, thank you for taking me for a walk around the park. What a beautiful night," she said, admirably.

"Any time. And I do mean that," he answered, looking down at her gaze with an affection that almost caused a loss of breath in his lungs.

As they approached a comfortable bench facing the beautiful view across Serpent Lake, he asked, "Maggie, could we sit for just a moment before I walk you back to your vehicle?"

She smiled happily and sat down.

Stuart held her mitten covered hand in both of his as they took breaths of cool air and cuddled close.

"Maggie. Such a sweet name. I like to say it out loud," Stuart whispered.

"You're silly, Stuart. The Cabernet got to your head." she laughed.

"Tell me about Samuel, Maggie."

She tensed into a tight statue of a human, frozen in the temperatures.

He took off his gloves and her mittens, then taking her hands between his -- he rubbed warmth into her.

"I mean it. I knew him, Maggie. But, not closely. And I know he was a good man. I admired him myself. I genuinely want to hear about the person Samuel was."

Maggie felt his question was just that – genuine. And she felt comfortable sharing the charming attributes that Samuel possessed, still keeping a few to herself.

"Hmmmmm, well, describing all that made up Samuel would take a whole night. But I will try to be concise…

Samuel was everything that is good in the world. He was giving. He was kind. He was patient. He was – wait? This sounds like a knock off of Corinthians 13."

Stuart smiled at her and lightly squeezed her hand, encouraging her to continue.

Maggie smiled, but stood up walking out to the edge between solid ground and the thick layer of ice on Serpent. Stuart followed a couple feet behind. Puffs of breath dissipated in front of her as she found the words to start again.

"The truth is Samuel was my true love, Stuart. I will never be able to deny that. From the moment I met him, I felt like, I don't know – wrapped in pure love, warmth, safety. He cared for me so perfectly, thought of my desires before they even occurred to me. He was fun, he was adventurous, witty, compassionate, stubborn, strong willed, handsome, and he loved his country and his duty. It is what took him in the end. I think I always knew, or felt, it would come to that. Though the blow was still something I wish I could forget. Oh, Samuel."

Maggie wrapped her arms around herself and looked out into the dark open space in front of her. She pictured summer afternoons when she and Samuel would take a picnic lunch out on his boat and fish for largemouth bass. He was always impressed by how, even with the fight the fish gave her, she could reel them in with the best of 'em. They would return home that evening, sunburnt and tired, but ready for a beer and fish fry while they sat on the deck listening to the loon calls and frogs chirping from nearby bogs. Such simple pleasures. The image in front of her faded and she found herself colder than moments ago.

Realizing even after sharing all she had with Stuart, that she still longed for his company, she turned around and rushed into his arms.

He held her without another word until she was ready to walk again.

CHAPTER 49

As she spent most mornings, Rose was busy in her kitchen. She hummed along with the radio as it played Kenny Rogers's version of *A Christmas Song*. She ladled bowls of steaming oatmeal into small ceramic bowls to serve to her guests, topping each with brown sugar, raisins and a generous pour of heavy cream. Lucille pulled the pans of bacon from the oven, the tantalizing smell filling the room. Jade and Sophia had finished their rice cereal moments earlier and were content to sit in their high chairs and watch the steady activity in front of them.

"Hi my sweethearts. You are being such good girls this morning," Rose said lovingly, stopping for a moment to kiss each baby on the cheek.

"Ok, Lucille. I'm going to take a tray of these dishes of oatmeal out to serve before the cream cools them too much. Follow me with the bacon and sliced cantaloupe when it is ready to go."

"Almost ready, Rosie," Lucille answered, after stealing a strip of bacon and taking a bite.

Rose snickered and backed out of the swinging kitchen door with her tray.

All rooms were occupied at *Simpler Times* and the dining room was full to capacity. It brought such joy to Rose to see her dream, a reality. Smiling faces gathered around her large dining room table, sipping coffee, discussing what shops to visit in town and how good the breakfast was smelling.

She started serving the bowls of oatmeal to each guest once Lucille entered the room with a cart carrying trays of bacon and a large oval platter of sliced ripe cantaloupe which she sat down in the center of the table between two tapered candles set in pewter candle holders. Rose carried a carafe of coffee around the table and refilled mugs. Lucille had set the trays of bacon on either side of the table for guests to serve family style. After the two agreed everyone looked content, they retreated back to the kitchen for the time being.

Walking down the hallway back to the kitchen, Rose put her arm through the bend of Lucille's.

"I will never get sick of seeing guests of my Inn gathered around the table enjoying their time here. Thank you for helping me do that, Lucille," Rose said with gratitude.

Lucille patted her hand as they walked.

"Rosie, I love it too. I am so happy to do so."

Smiling once more, Rose pushed open the kitchen door.

"Oh! Goodness Maggie! You scared me. I thought some intruder was sitting on the stool talking to my babies."

"I'm sorry! Marie let me in. I didn't want to disturb you as you waited on your guests, so I told her I'd keep the girls company for a few minutes," Maggie apologized.

"Oh no, no. Of course that is absolutely ok. I'm so glad you came. Anything you needed Maggie? Here, have a little bowl of oatmeal while you sit," Rose offered.

She had picked up such a habit from Mudsie of offering visitors food before they barely had a chance to say hello. Mudsie poured cups of coffee for diners at the café before they even ordered, brought over kettles of soup when she knew someone was unwell. Oh, how Rose missed her. It was a strange ache missing someone who had been a figment of her imagination. Though, she still knew in her heart her friends from Cherish were real. They lived. In another world? In another time? She never could make sense of it. But she had not only dreamed of Cherish. She had lived there, if only for a brief, wonderful time.

"Oh, well sure I guess. I haven't had oatmeal in such a long time. It smells delicious, Rose."

Lucille set a couple strips of bacon on a napkin next to Maggie, also. She reminded Rose of Mudsie too. She may have hired Lucille entirely from the nostalgic feeling she gave her, and completely ignored any kind of employment history.

"Mmm, thank you Lucille. Yum!" Maggie expressed, lifting a strip of bacon to her mouth and crunching loudly. "Oops, sorry. Not a dainty eater this morning I guess."

Rose laughed and started untying Sophia's bib.

"Tell me why you are beaming this morning. You are not the same lady I saw two days ago at *The Maple Leaf.*"

"Am I not?" Maggie asked. "Oh, thank you Lucille." She interrupted herself as Lucille filled her coffee cup.

"Rose, I think I wasn't only anxious about the letter and well, the meeting next week, but also the situation between Stuart and I."

Maggie took a bite of oatmeal and looked out the window for a moment.

"Well, I feel at peace, at least in that area," she stated, confidently.

Rose had just taken Jade's bib off too, but dropped it on the high chair tray when she heard Maggie's words.

"Rose! You knew Stuart and I would come together eventually. Didn't you? Let's just say we had a surprise meeting at the wine bar and it turned into more."

Rose plunked down on a stool and looked at her friend.

"More? What? Are you dating him, Maggie? Will this be 'Main Street official'?" Rose pried.

Maggie stood up and walked to the sink, setting her breakfast dishes inside.

"Rose, in this instant I am seeing the age gap between us for some reason." Maggie observed with a touch of humor in her tone.

"The truth is, he was interested in what I loved most about Samuel and asked, genuinely, about the man he was. Knowing he was well aware of my undying admiration for Samuel, and still wanted to be in my life, made me eager to have him be. And I began to appreciate the amazing man Stuart is too. I feel lucky."

Rose stood up from her stool and with both arms hugged her friend tight.

When she pulled back, both of her babies were starting to whimper, as if jealous of their mom's affections.

"Oh girls, you are fine. Maybe we need wiggle time on your blankets upstairs huh?"

As she lifted Jade out of the highchair, she turned to Maggie.

"My friend, I am so, so happy for you. And I know that no matter what you hear on your trip to DC, having Stuart's support will be a good thing. I feel there isn't anything they could share with you that would turn him away."

Lucille finished washing the few dishes from the sink and wiping her hands on her apron, started pulling Sophia out of her highchair.

"Thank you, Rose. My heart feels full. I kind of have a new peace that everything will be ok. I wanted to share that with a friend this morning."

"I'm so glad you did." Rose replied.

"Ok, I'm going to be on my way. Thank you so much for the breakfast. It was wonderful." Maggie said as she pushed through the kitchen door and left.

Rose looked at Lucille, each holding a squirming baby in their arms, and smiled with joy.

CHAPTER 50

TWO YEARS PRIOR

Samuel cracked his knuckles anxiously as he sat in the small waiting room. The nurse had told him it should only be a few minutes, yet he remained in the same chair still fidgeting thirty minutes later.

Tilman was healing well, but would be sent home in one month's time. Garcia had already gone back to his home in San Antonio, Texas with an honorable discharge. Unfortunately, and to Samuel's absolute anguish, Jose Garcia, had to have his left leg amputated from the knee down due to his injuries. Tilman would need time to heal from the burns he had sustained, but he luckily hadn't suffered any extreme disfigurement and the burn areas on his neck and arms were forming new skin that had blended well and though noticeable, would fade naturally within a few years. He too had been offered an honorable discharge as Garcia had, however, Nathan Tilman was already itching to return for the next mission.

The last sixteen days, Samuel would never forget. He, himself, had dealt with severe pains, though all were deep within his thoughts and emotions. The questions, the regrets, the self-blame, had taken over his mind so severely that he had no choice but to meet with a psychologist. As a career military officer, serving for over twenty years, just the mere act of scheduling an appointment with a psychologist had been difficult. Usually old fashioned, he was surprised to find that it wasn't an unusual thing to do. Since his first appointment, he had learned that several other fellow soldiers had taken the initiative to do the same. It took a special kind of courage to seek help. Samuel had accepted it, opened up and now was starting to feel the benefits. Prayer, for him, had always been a major source of strength and healing too. Without that, there just was nothing.

"Sergeant Ollweyes? You can come back now." A receptionist at the front counter said, waving him over.

Samuel stood up and straightened his cap.

"Thank you Miss Sira," he replied and walked down the hallway as he had done several times since the accident. Stopping at room 102, he breathed in a deep cleansing breath as Dr. Brown, his psychologist, had instructed him to. Pushing the door open, he noticed Zahra was sitting up, though he noticed even skinnier than the last time he had visited.

"Good morning, Zahra. How was your night's sleep?" he asked gently. He had personally hired a translator to be present when he visited, due to the language barrier. He had attempted learning the Dari dialect, however there were very little educational resources available. Even online and surprisingly the all-knowing Google had little information to give.

Kira, the Afghan translator, repeated what Samuel had asked.

Zahra nodded and smiled, her joy after seeing Samuel walk in, evident in her suddenly bright eyes.

Samuel grabbed a chair from the corner of the room and brought it over to the side of the bed, so that he could be close to Zahra.

"Are you feeling better today? I spoke with the doctor about giving you medication to help with the headaches and the nausea. Does it help much?" Samuel asked her, with a crease of real concern on his forehead.

Zahra turned to hear the translation from Kira, then turned back to Samuel. She slowly reached over and attempted a squeeze of his hand. The weakness in her frail embrace was noticeable and Samuel covered her hand with his.

She spoke words he didn't understand. They were few and not without physical effort.

He too looked to Kira for the words. As he heard them, his stomach dropped.

"Oh, no no. You are going to be ok, Zahra. Let's not discuss that just yet," he begged.

Gaining an unexpected strength, she pushed herself up on her bed and pulled Samuel closer. The act was superhuman almost, as he had not seen such determination and will from a sick, fading Zahra yet. She looked him in the eye and with an air of real conviction spoke for several minutes. Samuel could only comfort her while she did so, and show he was listening, even though the words were gibberish until Kira had translated them.

Trying to find the words in himself to reply, Samuel took a moment. In that moment he thought about Maggie. He missed her more than an explanation could capture. His home, the reality that was miles away, just didn't seem much more than a fairy tale he left behind, Maggie a perfect being he didn't deserve.

What Zahra asked of him – well, he didn't even know how to form a response upon his tongue. Because of his guilt, he felt he owed her the world.

But was it his to give? Or take, in this case?

CHAPTER 51

Maggie's stomach was sour. She wondered if she had eaten bad sushi from Yin's the night before. But, as it tended to do in life, reality set in shortly as she rubbed her eyes and looked at her phone. 3:00 a.m. shined brightly on her home screen. It also indicated only another three hours until her alarm clock went off. She would be driving to Minneapolis today, December 20th, boarding a plane destined for Washington DC, an apparent urgent meeting waiting on her attendance at the Pentagon. Rather peculiarly, the topic in which the discussion would be encompassing, was being kept silent. This fact, no doubt, annoyed Maggie, but it magnified her distress to unmanageable levels. Sleep was something she had been arduously attempting the last week, knowing her nerves and general health needed it. But, even with prescribed sleeping pills or nights of bubble baths and wine to sooth her, there was no use. The nightmares returned, the irritability with all who offered their help or kind words became commonplace and she had even asked Stuart to wait to contact her until the 23rd when she would be back in Crosby.

She laid awake for the next hour watching her and Samuel's life together in her mind like an old movie playing silently on a projector. It was almost soothing for a while, nostalgic. Maggie saw their days of dating in black and white. He was the handsome stranger in town, she was the young teenage girl serving ice cream at Cuyuna Soft Serve. Their wedding day flashed quickly through imaginary slides. As she walked down the aisle it was clear Samuel was up front waiting. And he was waiting calmly, firmly, confidently while he stared at his bride coming forward. It had struck her as very uncharacteristically groom like, but later found his composure at that moment to be the most admirable. It had proven his complete faith in their union and the love he had for Maggie.

She watched in the pitch dark of her bedroom as her memories played through her mind. Suddenly her alarm went off interrupting the movie. She had been so engrossed in the pictures flashing by, that she wasn't certain if she had fallen back asleep into a dream or if she was still just – remembering.

Either way, it was time.

Maggie pulled back the holiday hand-stitched quilt, swung her legs over the side of her bed and sat up. Taking a few minutes before committing to the efforts of the day, she said a few quiet words to God.

"Be with me," she simply said, and knew that He would.

CHAPTER 52

Maggie strategically packed the last remaining items into her carry-on suitcase. Moving her high heels to the side and rolling her pajamas tight, she squeezed in her tattered toiletry pouch she had purchased as a souvenir when she and Samuel went on a trip to Aruba, a mini travel fan and her fuzzy red slippers. As she closed the suitcase and zipped it shut, she thought she heard the doorbell. Thinking she was hearing things, she waited a few moments, listening. Who would be stopping this early in the morning? *Ding, dong.* There it was again. Unmistakable.

Maggie ran down the stairs to check who was at the door at this hour.

"Stuart? It's 7:00. What are you doing here?" she asked, surprised, but not disappointed.

"Well, I know we said our good-byes three days ago, but I couldn't sleep the last couple hours thinking of your travels," he answered, stepping inside and wiping his boots on the rug.

"Well, you and I both, Stuart. Please, come have a quick cup of coffee with me before I leave."

Maggie led him to the kitchen and poured coffee into one of her dainty white mugs, offering it to Stuart.

"Thank you, Maggie. But, listen, I didn't want to disturb you, but I felt something urging me to see you off this morning."

Maggie poured a bit more coffee in her cup and added a teaspoon of cream.

"Well, I am glad you did." She took a chance and reached over, squeezing his hand for a brief moment and smiled at him with appreciation.

She saw him swallow hard and blink away some feeling she couldn't place. Was it worry? Uncertainty? Regret? Guilt? Was he perhaps even falling in love with her and the very idea scared him? Again, she took another chance.

Maggie set her coffee cup down and walked close to Stuart, so close she felt his breath on her forehead. She put her hands on his chest and laid her head softly there. She felt him slowly bring his arms around her into an embrace.

Comfort. Support. Longing.

It was clear the two cared for one another. The hope that a lasting relationship was beginning seemed to be mutual. But, what if something changed after she returned? What was Maggie to learn at her meeting at The Pentagon?

She could feel the disquiet between them, even in their closeness.

"Maggie? I want you to know that I am here for you. I can imagine the anticipation of this day has brought you many sleepless nights and anxiety. But, I have faith that it will be ok. Something in me tells me, you will return to Crosby with closure, perhaps? Answers? Maybe even a letter or something Samuel had left behind? Something that will give you peace." He tilted her chin up so that she was forced to look him in the eyes.

"I can't make sense of why, but I feel it. And I send you with my love."

He kissed her lightly on the forehead, turned and walked toward the door. She stood there speechless, momentarily. His words made her ponder things in a new light. Why had she only expected sad news to be waiting for her when she reached her destination? Stuart gave her a new perspective just then.

"Stuart, wait!" She followed quickly and grabbed his hand.

"Thank you. Thank you so much for stopping this morning. I feel…I think…I am ready for whatever is put in front of me. I can face it. And I hope when I return, you are waiting for me."

"You can count on that, Maggie." he smiled, this time with confidence.

She closed the door behind him, watched his truck drive away and knew it was time to go.

CHAPTER 53

Rose sat at a booth in the Crystal Café with a cup of warm coffee between her still chilled hands. Steam was rising from her mug as other hungry patrons entered the restaurant, wiping their snow covered boots on the mat and locating an empty booth. Mudsie always kept a bustling and full house. Especially when it was a chilly Saturday morning.

"Sugar plum! So good to see you. Here, take this menu and scan it over, though I think you know it by heart don't you?" Mudsie said, smiling, as she scurried to the next table with menus and a coffee carafe.

Rose glanced up from her cup, looked around the room and out the window. She was confused. She saw the glass door and the old bell ding as families came inside. What was playing on the radio? She listened. *California Dreamin* by the Mamas and Papas? She noticed on the back wall near the restrooms, the pay phone, she herself had attempted several calls home on. Turning to peer out the window, she saw a 1955 Chevy Bel Air zip down Main Street. A couple of young boys threw snowballs from behind the cover of a mound of snow on the opposite side of the café where she sat. Women strolled with their hands snug in white muffs, their boyfriends holding tightly to their arm to prevent a slip on the ice in their pretty, yet impractical, American Duchess booties.

Rose couldn't make sense of this moment, why she was back in Cherish. But it felt comfortable and she missed it here so much. As she studied the menu a smile brightened her face. When was the last time she saw a #3 – two eggs to order, sausage links, bacon or ham, hash browns or home fries and an order of toast - $1.50. Well, the last time was when she was in this wonderfully happy town.

Mudsie returned.

209

"Ok, Rosie. What we having today?"

Rose stood up and wrapped her arms tightly around her plump, sweet friend.

"Oh Mudsie. I missed you so so much," she gushed.

Mudsie pulled back a bit and though she didn't usually shy away from hugs, she had a look of perplexity upon her wrinkly, but sweet face.

"Umm, baby girl – I sat at your kitchen table and shared a jelly donut with you two days ago. Ya miss me already?" Mudsie responded.

Rose realized, perhaps she was stuck in a dream, but she wanted, yearned, to hold on to it.

"Yes, Mudsie. I guess I do."

"Well, we will do it again soon. Now, what ya hungry for sister? The place is hoppin'!"

Rose sat back down, grinning at Mudsie's usual frankness.

"Ya know Mudsie, I am going to have your famous Swedish pancakes with strawberries and whipped cream. I feel like an extra special treat today."

"Ahhh, and you won't be sorry. Those are my personal favorites, Rose."

Mudsie grabbed the menu from Rose and scurried her order to the kitchen.

A mixture of smells escaped the kitchen as Mudsie pushed her way through the double doors. Salty fried bacon, sweet cinnamon rolls and savory sausage gravy were a few scents Rose could pick out. She hadn't realized how starving she was.

Her eyes continued scanning the dining area and noticed nothing had changed in her absence. Apparently there hadn't really been an absence, according to the comments Mudsie had shared earlier.

"Can I join you, Rose?" The words came from a man standing behind the booth Rose sat in. She recognized the voice, the kindest she had known, immediately. Taking a moment to hold on to her composure, she finally turned around.

"Father Eli! I would be honored to have you join me," she exclaimed, forgetting that it seemed no one else in Cherish seemed to know about her vanishing from their little town.

"Honored? How sweet, Rose. Well, thank you," Father Eli replied and slid into the booth seat opposite her.

Mudsie had noticed from behind the counter and rushed over a cup of coffee and a menu.

"Padre, what will ya have?" she asked, giving him less than ten seconds to scan the menu over.

"Mudsie, I think today I will have what Rose is having. She looks extra cheerful, and I bet it is because you are cooking up something special today."

Mudsie smiled at both of them and remarked, "There's a reason to celebrate something every day. And why not do it with Swedish pancakes huh?"

Rose watched her waddle away, but not without noticing her limp seemed a bit more pronounced. Mudsie would never in a hundred years admit her restaurant duties were over, but it was clear her body knew otherwise.

"So, Rose. How are things at the inn this holiday season? Keeping the rooms full?" Father Eli asked while folding his napkin over his lap.

Wondering how to respond without appearing completely taken aback, Rose decided to respond in truth, from how things were going in Crosby currently, at her inn.

"Well, yes we are full to capacity. And I am loving the holiday season there. A big tree in the sitting room, delicious meals served each evening and warm fires to enjoy all together before quiet time. It's a joy, Father. One you helped make happen."

Again, Rose was having a hard time separating her life in Cherish and her present life back in Crosby, *Simpler Times* flourishing in both places, eras, dimensions? How could she wrap her head around this?

"Oh, it was my pleasure, as I have told you time and time before. I had a feeling about you when I met you that spring day admiring the old yellow house. You saw your future. You were envisioning what you would make of it. Seeing you do that each day – well, it gives me real pride. You're so young and yet, you followed your dreams. I am, all of us here in Cherish – are happy for you, Rose." Father Eli looked back toward the packed booths and tables and suddenly all the faces were familiar and they were smiling at her with admiration and love. Chives, Daisy, Violet, Sully, Hank, Millie, all of her dear friends from Cherish, were here wishing her well.

"Father, I know this isn't real is it. A dream, I guess?" she asked, disappointment crossing her face.

He reached across the table gently taking her hand in his.

"Real? Is God real? Do you know that for certain? Perhaps Cherish is a place that lives in your heart, but I think some things you just need to find faith in. We can't try to make sense of things. But I feel your hand in mine at this moment."

"And I bet you are gonna taste the deliciousness in this pretty plate of Swedish pancakes!" Mudsie exclaimed, rushing out two heaping plates and setting them down in front of Father Eli and Rose, a strawberry slipping off the plate onto Rose's lap.

"Oh dang it, doll face. Let me get that." She wiped the strawberry off Rose's leg and dabbed it a bit.

"There we go! Better than ever." Mudsie said and folded her rag back into her apron pocket.

Rose frowned slightly.

"Not better than ever, Mudsie, but it will be ok."

Mudsie looked at Father Eli with a knowing look and her old eyes seemed sad. She kissed Rose on the forehead and continued to the next table with coffee for four. Tough as nails, sweet as pie – that was Mudsie.

"Well, I suppose we better taste this delightful breakfast that is almost too pretty to eat!" Father Eli suggested.

Rose took a scoop with her fork, being sure to get a portion of pancake, strawberry and whipped cream.

"Oh wow! This is amazing."

"I would have to agree." Father Eli responded.

After enjoying their breakfast in silence, Rose finally spoke.

"I hope this isn't the last I see of you all, Father Eli. The friends I have made here in Cherish, I just will never forget. You've all done so much for me. Truly."

"I know we will meet again, dear Rose. In the meantime, be the friend you need to be when others have dreams that are coming true or are reaching a path they desperately need help with. As you have experienced here in Cherish, nothing is of more value."

He set his fork down on his plate and covered it with the napkin from his lap.

"Rose, I will take care of the bill. You take a stroll down Main Street, Cherish. The fresh, cool air will do you good."

Hesitantly she stood up from her seat.

"Good bye, Father Eli."

CHAPTER 54

Maggie could scarcely breathe. Her flight had departed Minneapolis on time, she had located her suitcase immediately at baggage claim and after only twenty minutes of waiting her driver had arrived and was bringing her to Hotel Pentagon to get some rest and a meal, before her meeting in the morning.

For the first time in her travel experience, she wasn't sure she liked how quickly the trip had been. In a strange way she had wanted it to drag on, much like her and Samuel's trip to Maui, that not only was a nine hour flight, but had been delayed for six hours prior and their luggage then lost at their midnight arrival. At the time, she had sworn there was no destination worthy of that nightmare. But, rushing into an unknown, very official meeting, like she was scheduled to do in mere hours, didn't feel comfortable either.

"Here we are Mrs. Ollweyes. I will get a bellhop to come get your suitcase and bring you to your room. We have already checked you in and the concierge has your room number, key and anything else you may need." her driver informed as he opened the door for her.

"Oh, that won't be necessary. I only have this one suitcase. I can manage. Just point me in the right direction." Maggie answered. The gentleman stepped back, a bit surprised.

"Ok, yes Mrs. Ollweyes. No problem. There is the concierge's desk, just through the glass doors here. Give him this card and he will get you to your room. I will meet you down here in the same place at 8:00 a.m. sharp."

Maggie realized then, if the driver wasn't military, it was clear he worked for them. Direction was very straightforward.

"Thank you for taking such good care of me," she answered simply and turned to walk into Hotel Pentagon.

She had been polite, and handed her given card to the concierge who promptly had a bellhop show her to her room on the 27th floor overlooking all of Arlington, and some of DC in the distance. The view was amazing, though somehow she just wasn't feeling appreciative of the scenery.

Why was the unknown worse than a confirmed tragedy? Perhaps not, but it certainly was enough to make Maggie sick to her stomach. What reason did they have to not give her some kind of idea of why she was being "summoned" for lack of a better term? It didn't seem kind or frankly, respectful, to a career Army widow.

After purging the ginger ale and pretzels she had eaten on the flight, Maggie wiped her mouth and turned on the shower. Hot water pelting her body seemed like a good start, or at least an attempt, at a relaxing evening. She pulled her oversized sweater and leggings off, her undergarments and socks as well, and stepped carefully into the large spacious shower. Immediately she let the beads of water hit her face and trickle down her body. Surprisingly it helped melt away some of the anxiety she had built up over the course of the day. She lathered shampoo and then conditioner into her dark curls and finished with the lavender shower gel provided. The scents were soothing. She started to wonder if this was planned for fretful guests who were scheduled for unpleasant meetings at The Pentagon.

Taking her time under the warm streams calmed her tight muscles and suddenly Maggie was tired. It wasn't late. Was it even 5:00 p.m.? She didn't care. The bottle of water and raisin granola bar in her purse would be sufficient for dinner. And then if she fell asleep for the night, so be it. The quicker morning came, the better.

To be honest, she just wanted to rip off the proverbial band aid as soon as possible now that she was here. Why wait?

CHAPTER 55

As promised, Officer Royce pulled up in a black Nissan Maxima, with tinted windows and official plates, promptly at 8:00 a.m. in front of the hotel. Maggie had slept soundly for the first few hours of her early night, but the remainder was filled with unsettling dreams and frequent bouts of pacing the room. At 5:00 a.m. she had given up and started the coffee maker, grateful for the strong, quality coffee provided. After sipping the robust brew for an hour in front of the window, watching the city of Arlington, Virginia come to life, she decided it was time to prep herself. Hoping the shower would provide the same soothing effects it had done for her last night, she grabbed her clothes and walked to the bathroom.

"Mrs. Ollweyes." Officer Royce nodded as he opened the car door for her.

"Thank you, Officer. A beautiful day in Arlington, isn't it?" Maggie attempted usual pleasantries, despite her lack of enthusiasm for such.

"It seems so, Mrs. Ollweyes," he answered in a short, but polite response. No doubt, even this type of assignment, he had been trained for.

On the short drive, Maggie watched out her car window at vehicles passing by, the clouds in the blue sky and the massive, intimidating structure they were nearing. Despite being married to an Army Sergeant who had served for over twenty years, she still had never actually been to The Pentagon. Though it was well known as the headquarters for the United States Department of Defense, most officers, even many of the top commanding officers, did not work directly at The Pentagon. Something made her wish she would have at least taken a tour with Samuel. Perhaps now, as they edged closer and closer, wouldn't have quickened her breathing so, had she been there prior. Maggie dug in her oversized leather purse for her water bottle, suddenly feeling parched and warm, despite the winter weather.

"Mrs. Ollweyes, are you ok? We can make a stop, should you need one," Royce offered, glancing in his rearview mirror at Maggie.

Embarrassed that her agitation was noticeable, but knowing there was no way to hide it, she decided to be real.

"I am just nervous. Nothing more than that, Officer. I, well, I can't begin to guess what all of this is about. And after what I went through a year ago, it unsettles me a great deal. I'm sure you can understand." She replied with raw honesty.

"I do, Mrs. Ollweyes. I wish I could reply with a comforting assurance that all will be well. However, I don't know the subject of the meeting. Only, my direction. But, I do wish you well. And though I didn't know your husband personally, I have heard from many that he was one of the best." Officer Royce added, with admiration in his words.

Maggie managed a soft smile.

"Thank you."

"Ok, here we are." he added, as they turned onto Washington Boulevard, accessing the gates to The Pentagon.

As they pulled up to a marked parking spot, Officer Royce put the car in park and sat in silence for a few moments, knowing Maggie needed to do the same.

"Mrs. Ollweyes, Officer Sheffield will meet us at the entrance and then he will take you to a meeting room on the second floor. I am not certain if Captain Stanley will be present or who will be in attendance. All I know is I have brought you here, and now, with no further information to share, I will say goodbye."

Again, Officer Royce was polite, but very business-like. Something about this young soldier reminded her of Samuel years ago. Her heart was both melancholy and proud.

"What's your first name, soldier?" She asked without thinking.

"Daniel, ma'am." he answered.

"Well, Daniel, thank you for serving our country. I can see, even at a young age, you are doing your job very well. Your parents, no doubt, are very proud."

"Thank you, Mrs. Ollweyes. I believe they are," he smiled at her, before opening his door and walking around the back of the vehicle and doing the same to hers.

Maggie took one more deep breath, and stepped outside. A sudden gust of breeze whispered through her hair like the small table fan on her night stand, and then was gone. It was fleeting, but she noticed it. Was he near? He filled her heart at that moment, she knew that much. And suddenly, she felt ready for whatever was next.

"Officer Royce, thank you soldier. You can report back to base." Officer Sheffield said, and then turned his full attention to Maggie.

"Mrs. Ollweyes, it's an honor to have you here today. I know it has been over a year now since Samuel's passing, but I assure you, hardly a day goes by that I don't think of him for a brief moment. He and I were close. We served closely together, as you know."

Maggie shook his hand and replied, "I do know, Officer. And I too find my thoughts on him often." She smiled softly at him.

"Naturally. At any rate, he was a good man," he replied and continued. "Well, shall we? Right this way to the elevator. Captain Stanley was able to make the trip as he had hoped. Another longtime friend and fellow soldier to Samuel. There may also be others in attendance but we will meet them a little later. Ok, here we are."

Officer Sheffield pushed the elevator button to go up to floor two.

Maggie wondered who else would be present at the meeting and why. Although, she realized, why speculate, she had not a clue what she had been called here for in the first place.

CHAPTER 56

TWO YEARS PRIOR

S amuel held Zahra's frail hand between both of his, knowing her last breath was near. He had visited more times than he could count in these last two months, hoping and praying, but it seemed God had other plans.

"Zahra? Can you hear me?" He spoke softly to her, his eyes welling up with tears he was fighting to hold back.

Kira stood at the other side of the bed and translated Samuel's words.

Zahra didn't open her eyes, but she turned her head in Samuel's direction and nodded.

She was such a beautiful woman. Even when her body had deteriorated to sickly skin and bones, her hair still had luster like the moon's shine on a midnight river, her skin was as smooth as satin and until mere hours ago, her spirits were as positive and bright and full of faith as Samuel had ever seen. He had so much admiration for her. He had never seen a human so strong and determined.

"Zahra, listen to me. I want you to know you can go anytime you need to. Do not worry. All will be ok here, taken care of. I promise. Please, for once in your life, have peace."

Kira sniffled, but spoke the words very clearly.

Zahra smiled and her hand slipped from Samuel's, allowing herself to go.

CHAPTER 57

"**M**rs. Ollweyes, Maggie, Good to see you." Captain Stanley greeted, standing up from his desk. He quickly rounded the side of his desk and reached for her hand.

"Thank you so much for making the trip, especially at this time of year. I apologize that this process has taken so very long. You wouldn't imagine the red tape." he continued.

She glanced at Officer Sheffield, with a momentary look of confusion. *Am I supposed to know what he is talking about?*

"Here, Maggie, let's take a seat over this way." Officer Sheffield suggested, anxiously. He led her to a leather arm chair in a spacious sitting area in Captain Stanley's large office.

Though being in The Pentagon was itself an unimaginable experience, and an official meeting such as this hard to prepare for, she found the area she was sitting now to be very inviting and comfortable. Admittedly, she expected to be sitting in a conference room at a large table with papers and files being shoved at her filled with sheets of paper covered in tiny print that she didn't understand, but ultimately added up to the fact that her husband was still dead, not coming back, and why keep rubbing her face in it?

But, her comfortable chair faced a large window that looked out across a grassy courtyard where tourists and history buffs read plaques about American history and sat on memorial benches, relishing the view of the building from which she sat.

"May I get you a cup of coffee, a bottle of water, juice, tea?" a woman asked, approaching Maggie as she gazed out the window. She was dressed in a white silk blouse and a navy pencil skirt. Her hair was pulled back tight and simple, pearl earrings the only jewelry she wore.

Maggie cleared her throat.

"I, um, yes, I would love a cup of coffee, with cream if you have it?" she asked.

"Yes, of course, Mrs. Ollweyes." The woman asked and left the room swiftly.

Maggie wasn't sure if Officer Sheffield and Captain Stanley left her to sit on her own by design, or if their discussions were unintentionally delaying the actual meeting at hand. Either way, she appreciated it. Though still apprehensive for whatever was to come, she was content to sit in her chair and admire the room before her and the courtyard out front. Something about a place that worked for and honored soldiers like her husband, gave her a sense of pride and a glimpse of what Samuel felt for his country. To experience a piece of it made his death seem like it wasn't in vain.

"Here you are, Mrs. Ollweyes."

Maggie turned to see a pewter tray with a white porcelain cup and saucer, a small pewter coffee carafe and a mini pitcher of cream in front of her. Her server poured the cup full of coffee and added a touch of cream. She laid a spoon on the saucer and handed Maggie a white cloth napkin.

"Is there anything else I can get you Mrs. Ollweyes?"

"I think this is sufficient. In fact, this is lovely. Thank you very much." Maggie responded and stirred her coffee, watching the cream swirl into the dark browns of the coffee.

The woman smiled, and nodding simply, left the room.

Maggie took a sip of her coffee and set the dainty cup down on the saucer again, with a little clink atop the China. Something about drinking coffee from a small China cup and saucer made it taste that much better. For whatever reason, she was feeling better here. She was feeling ok. Like Samuel was here with her somehow. She knew he wasn't, but this was his world, not hers, and she felt him.

"Mrs. Ollweyes, can we join you?" Captain Stanley asked, startling her a bit.

"Oh, gosh. Yes, of course. I was just admiring your courtyard out front. It appears to be a beautiful memorial to our fallen soldiers." She smiled, nodding toward the window.

"It is, indeed. You should take a stroll through before you leave. I find that it brings much comfort to loved ones who have lost someone while serving. Truly, you will believe, they did not die in vain." Captain Stanley spoke with pride.

"At any rate, Maggie. How have you been?" he asked, switching gears.

"Well…" she started, pausing to find the right words.

"I'm sorry. I know that is something you hear often and is probably not the easiest question to answer, truth be told," he added, with compassion.

"Yes, you are correct. I guess, Captain, all in all, I am doing well. As you can imagine, the first several months I found it difficult to get out of bed or to pour a cup of coffee. But it's amazing how time does in fact heal. Though, I feel Samuel helping me every day."

Maggie picked up her cup and saucer and took another sip of her coffee, if for no other reason than to have a distraction to hold off the sudden moisture forming in the corner of her eyes.

"He was one of the best, Mrs. Ollweyes. You should know he is greatly missed here as well," Captain Stanley told her.

"Very much so." Officer Sheffield added.

"Thank you, both." she replied.

Maggie set her cup and saucer back down on the tray in front of her and waited a few moments before speaking, hoping perhaps the gentlemen would move along with the urgent matters of the called meeting today.

"Yes, well Maggie, let's get to it." Captain Stanley walked back to his desk and grabbed a file thick with documents. Officer Sheffield sat in one of the arm chairs across the tea table from Maggie. After Captain Stanley joined them, he asked, "Maggie, do you know why we called this meeting?"

"Captain, I haven't a clue. Though my imagination has gone wild." Maggie attempted to make things light, her tone unconvincing.

"Ahh, well, I'm afraid there may be some shocking information we will need to share with you. This file in my hand contains all there is to know."

Maggie's eyes automatically moved down to the file he held tightly in his hand, *CLASSIFIED* stamped in red on the cover.

"I don't understand. Did Samuel do something wrong?" her tears threatened to start again.

Captain Stanley looked at Officer Sheffield with a silent agreement forming between the two as she waited.

"Listen, I think what would be best is for you to take this file back to your hotel room and read through it yourself. It isn't the customary way to do these things, however, neither is this whole matter. I know we can count on your discretion and safekeeping of the file."

"Yes, of course. But, what do I do once I have – I don't know – completed the task?" she asked, anxiety building again.

"We will wait for your call, Mrs. Ollweyes."

Captain Stanely walked the file over to Maggie and as if it was made of paper thin glass she carefully took it from him and slipped it in her oversized purse, zipping it shut.

"Your driver will be here shortly, Maggie."

CHAPTER 58

Before Maggie got off the elevator she noticed Officer Royce waiting by the front entrance. Each step she took her legs shook a bit, beads of perspiration were forming at her temples. Her right hand held tight to the file in her purse. This felt like a movie, like a weird conspiracy or something. Though, it did occur to her that her imagination was getting the better of her again.

"Mrs. Ollweyes, I am to take you back to the hotel, correct?" Officer Royce asked.

"Yes, please. Right away."

"Mrs. Ollweyes, are you all right?" he asked, noticing her flushed cheeks and the troubled look in her eyes.

"I think so. I just would like to get back and take a nap, call home, check on things. You know how it goes."

He wasn't convinced, but nodded in agreement.

The entire drive back to the hotel her mind was reeling. *Did Samuel do something illegal? Was his death not as swift and painless as she had been informed? Was there some unfinished business concerning her husband?* Evidently so, or she wouldn't be here.

"Here we are, Mrs. Ollweyes," Officer Royce said, when they reached the hotel. Maggie hadn't noticed until that moment that he had kept silent the entire ride, sensing she was deep in her thoughts.

"Thank you Officer. I suspect we may see each other again tomorrow?" she asked as he opened the door for her.

He nodded. "It is very possible."

After Maggie unlocked the door to her room, walked in and set her purse down, she almost didn't know what to do. Was she ready to open the file and sift through the obvious stack of documents inside? The circumstances of the meeting she had just left seemed quite unusual. Did they typically just give a classified file to a family member and let them drive away from the premises? Bizarre, really. Though, she knew Samuel, Officer Sheffield and Captain Stanley had been extremely close and their trust in her discretion was unequivocal. Perhaps, too, they felt this was the best way to deliver "the blow" so to speak – Maggie paging through things as she felt manageable, digesting it as she went on.

Feeling annoyed with her very own anxiety, Maggie decided to set the file on the desk, unopened for now and take a walk. She needed some cool air and deep breaths of it. She needed time to just walk and think and be, for a bit.

Changing into her tennis shoes, fleece leggings and an oversized down pull-over, Maggie almost ran out of her room, down to the lobby and out the large glass sliding doors.

Oh, the cool air felt exhilarating. She took a left and continued on for a few blocks. Her pace picked up to a comfortable jog. Still she kept on. Something about the exertion was absolutely what she needed to give her the energy and the confidence to do what she had to do this evening. Her lungs burned, but it felt good. She hadn't run in a few years, but now felt like the right time.

After several miles weaving through intersections and city blocks, she was back to her hotel. A meal and a warm shower sounded good.

Maggie sat at the small table in her hotel room sipping on a glass of burgundy. She swirled a few noodles around her fork and took a bite of the Spaghetti Carbonara she had ordered from room service. She wasn't hungry, but having eaten next to nothing today, she felt it was wise to put something in her body. The wine maybe wasn't a good idea before her heavy task at hand, but she decided one glass may calm her nerves. Despite her lack of appetite the creamy sauce covered noodles and the smoky saltiness of the pancetta generously sprinkled over top was extremely tasty. Maggie took a few more bites, and laid her cloth napkin over the half-eaten meal, feeling guilty for the waste. Taking another sip of the dark red wine, clearly top shelf she decided while swirling it in her mouth, she thought about calling home. Would Rose or Flynn have any advice on how to proceed with what she needed to do? Or could they at the very least be morale support while she opened the file, perhaps revealing something troubling? Calling Stuart, though she yearned for his ability to comfort her and be held, it was not an appropriate time. She knew then who to call. Even if the person she was dialing was elderly and sometimes she tried Maggie's patience, Mom was always there for her through thick and thin.

After a few rings, Maggie worried perhaps her mom had gone to bed early.

"Hello Margaret. How are you my sweet girl?" Sarah, Maggie's mother, answered.

"Mom, you are the only person that calls me Margaret. But, I am ok. How are you?" She replied, hoping in vain that her mom wouldn't pick up on the stress in her tone.

"What's the matter? I know the holidays have been difficult since Samuel's death. Is that it?" Sarah asked.

How does she do that?

"To be honest, Mom, I am in Arlington, Virginia. I can't believe I'm saying this, but I had a meeting at The Pentagon today. Something came up regarding Samuel. I don't know what just yet. It's all right here in front of me and I can't... I... I'm scared." The tears Maggie had been holding back began to flow. She laid her phone down and laid her head in her hands, letting herself crumble. Even though Maggie's phone was on speaker, it was silent. Sarah, let her daughter have the moment she needed. After several, Maggie grabbed a few tissues from her purse and blew her nose and dabbed under her eyes. Breathing in and out and in and out slowly, she returned to the conversation that had barely begun.

"Mom? Are you still there? I'm sorry. I lost it for a minute."

"You did. That's good. You needed it. Good Lord, you *have* to lose it sometimes Margaret. No one can keep it together all the time. You have been through so much this past year. And evidently something more has been dropped at your feet?" Sarah asked, a forced strength in her voice.

"That's just it, Mom. I don't know, yet. I have a file here that I can't bring myself to open."

"Maggie, take another good swallow of your wine and grab the file." Sarah told her.

Maggie, a grown adult of 43, did what her mother had ordered, without acknowledging the obvious reasons she no longer needed to abide by them.

Draining the last third of her glass of wine, Maggie reached in her purse on the floor and pulled out the file Captain Stanley had entrusted her with. It was inches thick. What could've happened that such accumulation of documents was necessary?

"Ok, it is sitting here in front of me, mom. Now what?" she asked, hoping for some miraculous words of strength from Sarah.

"You open it. Just you honey. Say a little prayer if you wish. But find the strength. And I know you hate this, but I promise you, it will be ok."

Sarah gave Maggie a minute to respond.

"Ok, Mom. I will. I love you." Maggie said and was glad she had called.

"I love you too. Good night."

Maggie waited for her mom to hang up and when she physically saw the call had ended, she set her phone down, switched the ringer to silent and delicately, as if it may break, she grabbed the front of the file and opened it.

CHAPTER 59

Rose poured a ½ cup of dry cat food into the tin dish and filled the other with cool water from the bathroom faucet for Muffin. She was taking care of *The Maple Leaf* tenant while Maggie was away.

"Here you go kitty. I bet you are missing Maggie, aren't you Muffin?" Rose spoke softly while she scratched behind the cat's ears.

Rose checked the storage room, the office kitchen combo room, behind the counter and all over the display room of the store before flipping the light switches and locking the doors to *The Maple Leaf*.

Maggie had hired a very part-time employee, Kate, a year ago, after Samuel's death. At the time it felt necessary as some days she found it almost impossible to even lift her head from the pillow she laid upon.

But since, Maggie had really been grateful for Kate's willingness to come in from time to time. She had been able to leave for weekends to visit her mother and attend the occasional trade show out of town to find new and unique pieces for her shop.

Kate had worked until 3:00 p.m. and closed, but Rose still liked to check on *The Maple Leaf* and lonely little Muffin before she put the twins to bed.

She took one more glance at Muffin staring out the window as she started her walk back to *Simpler Times*.

Rose wondered what Maggie was doing at that moment. Did she find out why the urgency in the meeting? Had she been given some news that brought back raw and painful memories? Rose looked up at the clear sky, a black canvas, a silver crescent moon peeking through. A shiver ran down her spine for a moment. It wasn't from the chill in the winter air, but a memory of her own. She thought back to the night she ended up in Cherish and how it had started.

Flynn had been deployed and after their house had sold, she had been staying with her mom and dad temporarily. One evening as they watched the news, headlines concerning the war in Afghanistan covered the screen, even footage of the wreckage. When statistics of US soldier casualties popped up on the screen, Rose could no longer take it. She had run out to her car through torrential rains looking for some sort of escape. Her heart had been beating fast, her breathing labored. She felt on the edge of a nervous breakdown, the fear for her husband's life sending her into a downward spiral. She had driven for hours and ended up in a town called Cherish. The town had arguably changed her whole life. But that was another story.

As Rose walked down Main Street she saw Clem in his store sweeping the floors. He looked up as she walked by the window and waved. She smiled and felt so grateful. This life she now led – it was more than she deserved.

But part of her felt the ache of unwarranted guilt. *Why had someone like Maggie, so giving and selfless, not been given a child like she had been? Blessed with twins even. Why did a kind person such as Maggie have to lose her husband who had fought for his country just as Flynn had?*

Rose could see her home, her inn, *Simpler Times*, in the distance as she turned the corner down 3rd Street. As she neared the festively decorated, turn of the century two story, she called home, a sudden answer came to mind. Faith. The only way to make sense of absolutely everything in this life was to just plainly keep faith, have faith, *find* faith if you feel it is far from your grasp. Rose remembered her days in Cherish had been filled with prayer and dependence, *faith* in God's plan. There was never a point in trying to make sense of things and now she needed to believe it and be there for her friend, no matter what news she came back with.

Rose stepped onto her wooden porch and saw the glowing Christmas tree through the living room window. She smiled and knew somehow Maggie was going to be ok.

CHAPTER 60

Maggie knew it was time. She had cleared her dinner dishes from the table and replaced her glass of wine with a bottle of water. The open file sat in front of her, the stack of papers waiting to be read.

Closing her eyes she took a deep breath in and as she exhaled slowly she looked down at what sat in front of her. As suspected there were several tabs in various colors separating documents into categories. Some were labeled with words she would need to Google such as 'Apostille', 'Dossier' and several acronyms like USCIS and IAA.

She fanned through the first few pages just trying to pick out something that had Samuel's name on it or could give her a clue of what these many pages of tiny print and official stamps meant to her. How was she involved? She noticed a few pages stapled together, Samuel's signature at the bottom of the last page next to another signature. She couldn't make out the signature at all, but the name was printed underneath – Zahra. Only a first name? And who was this person, this Zahra?

Maggie began to feel an uneasy tightening in her chest. She stood up and took off her sweater, only a tank top underneath. She opened her water bottle and took a long drink.

What is this? What am I about to read?

Deciding to cut to the chase, Maggie grabbed her phone and pulled up Google on the screen. She started with *Apostille*. The meaning was lengthy, but basically pertained to a certificate of the authentication of a document in another country. That didn't give her much information really. She tried *Dossier*. The meaning a bit more precise this time, indicating it being a set of documents used for an international adoption to assign guardianship or adoption of a child from a foreign country. Maggie reread the meaning again more slowly. What could this have to do with Samuel?

Forcing herself to remain calm to avoid panic, she typed in the acronym USCIS. United States Citizenship and Immigration Services. Typing as fast as she could she entered IAA. The Intercountry Adoption Act.

Adoption?

Maggie looked at the front of the stapled documents containing Samuel's signature and of this stranger – Zahra. On the front of the legally binding document, the embossed seal depicted the national emblem of Afghanistan. A judge's official stamp was also included on the document as well as that of a US military attorney.

What Maggie gathered from the bits and pieces she was pulling from the puzzle was, startlingly, her husband had adopted or took over guardianship of an Afghan child while he had been stationed there.

The reasons why – still a complete mystery to her.

And that she had received not a word of this until almost two years later – a shock that would be hard to recover from.

CHAPTER 61

Maggie hadn't slept well, but woke at 6:00 a.m. and went straight to the shower. Again, she relished in the lavender scented soaps and stood for twenty minutes straight letting the warm water soak her body. She felt – well, the truth was, she couldn't define what she was feeling. She had read enough to know that Samuel had taken on the responsibility of a child, an Afghan child. She couldn't begin to even imagine how this had come about. She was almost scared to know.

An imagination can do crazy things to one's brain. She envisioned Samuel having an affair with this woman and feeling responsible for her child. In every single angle she looked at it, the scenario was just plain wrong. It was perfidy. It was of the utmost deceitfulness. It was simply unfaithful. *None* of which were Samuel. She would go to her grave believing and standing by that.

Something had happened. Something which caused him to feel utterly responsible.

Maggie finished rinsing the conditioner from her hair and turned the water off. She had sifted through the file enough. It was all legal documentation. She wanted some real answers. She dried off and wrapped her body in the plush white bath towel. Tucking her toes into the slippers provided complimentary by the hotel, she shuffled out to retrieve her phone from the nightstand.

After only two rings, Officer Sheffield answered.

"Good morning Mrs. Ollweyes. I gather you read through the file?"

"Good morning Officer. I did and I didn't. The file is filled with legal small print that I frankly don't understand and don't have time for. I found enough information to give me a clue of what is going on here. After dealing with the shock, I really just would like some answers. Do you have any for me? Does Captain Stanley? Does Zahra? I can't make sense of this. If it had been under different circumstances, perhaps I, myself, would've been open to adoption. But, my husband is gone and this is, I don't understand why, or what could have possibly happ..."

Finally Maggie's wall collapsed, at least at this weak moment. She didn't know why now, but Officer Sheffield was the unlucky recipient of her melt down.

Maggie set her phone down on the bed and laid down hugging the pillow to her chest, her body retching with each breath, tears streaming down her cheeks.

A baby, a child. Her one true wish, what she grew up thinking was her purpose in this world – to be someone's mama. But, Samuel was gone. They had tried so hard to have a baby. Why did he do this? And what was she to do about it? So many emotions consumed her while she lay, and they all poured out saturating the pillow she held tight.

After ten minutes she felt more tired than she had last night. Her head pounded and her eyes felt swollen and itchy. She figured by now Officer Sheffield had hung up, but she grabbed her phone off the plush comforter anyway and brought it to her ear.

"Officer Sheffield? Shawn?"

"I'm here, Mrs. Ollweyes. I'm so very sorry you have to go through this. I too, though not in comparison, had finally put Samuel's death to rest. So digging those feelings up and this news thrown at you? Well, I can imagine you are distraught." he answered kindly.

"Yes. I'm not sure how to process this. Though, I feel perhaps with some type of explanation or background – I may start to? Can we meet again today and discuss things further? You must have some information that you can share?" She asked.

"I will bring this to the Captain, Maggie. We will plan on Officer Hayes picking you up at 10:00 a.m.? Will that work?" Officer Sheffield replied.

"Yes, that will be fine. I'm going to rest an hour and then restart the day. Thank you, sir. I will see you soon."

Maggie pushed the *end* button and set her phone on the nightstand. She then rolled over and fell fast asleep.

After a few minutes with her eyes closed the unmistaken scent of Samuel's cologne seeped into her nostrils. Such a clean, manly, comforting smell.

"Hi Maggie."

She felt his soft hand caress her cheek, then run a few fingers through her damp hair. When she opened her eyes, he was there. As plain as day, he sat on the side of the hotel bed looking down at her with love and longing in his.

"Samuel."

She smiled and grabbed his hand, kissing it time and time again, and holding it to her cheek so tight, that perhaps he wouldn't fade like he always did.

"I'm sorry I can't be with you right now, my love." he apologized.

"Please. I would do almost anything, Samuel, to have you come back. This isn't fair."

Though Maggie knew. She knew there was nothing she could do about the past or to make sense of why it happened like it did.

"I know. I promise you, I had always intended to come home and live this out with you. That's all I ever wanted. God works in mysterious ways, sometimes vexingly so. Still, trust in it. Trust in accepting new love and trust in *letting it go*." Samuel smiled with a happiness she wasn't expecting. Like...He wanted her to move on.

"Samuel," she whispered.

"I love you Maggie."

CHAPTER 62

"**M**a'am," Officer Hayes said, tipping his cap and opening the car door for her.

"Good Morning, Officer." She said simply. She had slept for an hour after her phone call to Officer Sheffield, though she still felt unrested. The file was tucked again, safely, in her oversized purse, all documents snug inside. She was hoping for a more informal, a less wordy, explanation to what she had discovered. *Why, Oh why, had Samuel felt the need to take on full responsibility for a child? What were the circumstances?* She just wanted to know a basic answer to this question first and then try to form additional questions in her head.

The vehicle pulled up to a building that was not, clearly not, The Pentagon.

"Officer Hayes, why are we stopping here?" she asked.

"Mrs. Ollweyes, this is the Arlington location for the USCIS. Your meeting will be held here today," he answered.

She remembered reading about the USCIS in the paperwork last night. Given the information included, this seemed like a logical place to meet.

"Here we are, Mrs. Ollweyes," Officer Hayes said, opening the door for her again.

"Thank you. I imagine I will see you at meeting's end?" she asked, seeing he wasn't motioning to follow her into the building.

"That is a good possibility."

He climbed back into the driver's seat, shut his door and merged into busy city traffic.

A tiny part of her wished he would've stayed and guided her to where she needed to be. But she knew the answer would become clear soon. Afterall, she was in this alone, whether she wanted to be or not. And as she watched the taillights of that black Nissan Maxima fade into the distance, she knew.

It was time to be strong, accept things as they were, and find faith in herself to do so. She didn't even know if it mattered anymore what had happened. She knew Samuel enough to know that he felt strongly about this, *needed to do this,* and he had felt certain she would be completely supportive.

Maggie stood a minute longer until she could see Officer Hayes's car no more.

Turning toward the building she noticed two men sharply dressed walking toward her, and recognized them right away.

"Mrs. Ollweyes. Good morning. Let us walk with you to where today's meeting will be held," Officer Sheffield offered. Captain Stanley nodded in agreement.

Again, they walked through large sliding glass doors and down a very clean, very quiet hallway. After passing several closed doors, they came to an open one where a middle aged woman stood waiting. She looked, well Maggie wasn't well educated in ethnicities, but she appeared to have bloodlines in India, or perhaps the Middle East. Maggie was embarrassed to even speculate as perhaps the two were as opposite as they come.

The woman greeted them with a strong accent. Again, Maggie couldn't begin to guess where she was from. She was short, maybe 5 ft 2 in, dark skin, fine features, shiny black hair and stocky. She wore bright gold earrings and a colorful satin blouse that was oversized and hung below her hips where she wore black slacks.

"Mrs. Ollweyes, It's a pleasure to finally meet you." she said, smiling at Maggie and gently shaking her hand.

"Yes, likewise, Ms.?" Maggie questioned.

"Mina Patel."

"Beautiful name. Well, great to meet you Mina."

"Right this way." She offered, pointing them to a round table in the center of the room.

Sitting on the round table was a stack of paperwork kept together by a large binder clip, three pens sat perpendicular to the papers, a potted purple African violet sat in the center of the table. Six chairs sat around the table. Maggie noticed a counter against the far wall that held a Keurig coffee maker, cups, and stir sticks. A pitcher filled with water sat just to the left.

A bit surprising, in the corner of the room, was a wooden toy box. Sitting next to it was a large rug with colorful zoo animals woven into it. Blocks sat in disarray on top, as did a few baby dolls and toy cars. A child sized table and two chairs were pushed against the wall just to the right of the toy box and it appeared an interrupted puzzle sat on the table waiting to be completed.

Maggie's face flushed, which didn't escape Mina's studying eye.

"Here, please sit Mrs. Ollweyes. Let me get you a glass of water."

Officer Sheffield pulled out one of the cushioned chairs for Maggie and she sat down.

All in attendance did the same while Mina delivered a glass of water to each of them.

"Ok, Mrs. Ollweyes. I think you have grasped, for the most part, what Samuel had committed to many months back. Though we do not have all the answers you wish to hear, we do have some basic information."

Maggie sipped her water and nodded, listening intently.

"Officer Sheffield can attest to a mission he and Samuel were on together that did not end the way they had intended. Even sharing that information is classified and can't be shared after leaving this office."

Again, Maggie continued to listen.

"It was confirmed though, that an Afghan family had been seeking shelter in the building where the soldiers were searching for Taliban members. Samuel was the commanding officer, the leader of this particular mission. Well, something went wrong and the family was injured when a grenade had mistakenly gone off. Two soldiers also sustained severe injuries."

Maggie cut in. "I don't understand where this is going. What does this have to do with Samuel adopting a child?"

"Mrs. Ollweyes, the family was transported to the local hospital, but the husband, Amad, died soon after having taken the blow of the fallen rock from the ceiling while protecting his wife and child. The wife, Zahra, lasted for several weeks, but she weakened more and more each day. Samuel came every single day to check on her and the child. Zahra tried with every inch of energy she could to stay alive for her baby, but when she knew her last breath was nearing – she asked Samuel for the utmost favor. Such a request is typically unthinkable, especially in a country such as Afghanistan. But Zahra had no family left, she feared deeply for her child in a war torn land. She could see the kindness in Samuel's eyes and she knew her child would be taken to the United States and live a healthy life full of love. That was her last wish, as any mother's would be, to know her child was safe and cared for."

"Though I am proud of Samuel and, well, if it's possible, find even more admiration for him after hearing this, um – did he just say "yes" without a second's hesitation? Without sending word to me asking for my blessing, my support, my commitment to this life changing decision?"

The room was quiet for a minute. Ms. Patel, Officer Sheffield and Captain Stanley gave Maggie time to digest what she had heard.

"Mrs. Ollweyes, Maggie, sometimes looking into the face of pure desperation, compassion knows not a simpler solution can be found." Mina said finally, breaking the silence gently.

Maggie stood up from her chair and walked over to the window, setting her glass of water on the window sill. The sun was shining on the light dusting of fresh snow, the sidewalk was busy with people rushing here and there, a hand holding a cell phone to their ear, a coffee in the other. Life kept on, the hustle and bustle of the day continued as she sat silent in a world she was not expecting.

Maggie looked up from the sidewalks in front of her and saw a church in the distance. It was a few blocks away, but the tall exquisite steeple caught her eye, a cross perched at the very tip. She stared at it for a very long time. Find faith she had heard time and time again this last many months. Not have faith, but find faith. Perhaps she had.

Clearing her throat finally, Mina spoke. "Maggie? Would you like to see a photo?"

Maggie turned and walked back to the table.

"Yes, I think I would."

EPILOGUE

Maggie sat next to Stuart holding his hand with her left hand, slicing a bite of lemon bundt cake with the other. Rose had set a lovely Easter table with a total of twenty five friends and family gathered around. It was an unseasonably warm April day and Flynn had opened a few windows. The birds were chirping outside and a light breeze tickled the tiny buds on the tree branches. Stuart looked at Maggie and smiled. They were both so happy and truly in love. Maggie knew she would never stop loving her Samuel, but she had said goodbye and felt in her heart it was ok now.

Jade started to cry in the corner of the room where a few toys had been set up for the girls to play with.

"Jade, you're ok. Here, hold your Peppa pig doll." Rose told her affectionately after Sophia took ownership of the maracas she had been shaking. Rose tucked a tiny curl behind Sophia's ear and patted Jade on the head, smiling with all the love in the world.

Maggie admired the love Rose had for her daughters and now, by the grace of God, by his mysterious plan, Maggie could relate wholeheartedly.

She set her fork down and gazed at her daughter playing with the box of blocks on the floor. She studied each shape so carefully, and when one wouldn't fit into the hole in the box, she wouldn't give up. There was determination in the crease of her forehead, the steadiness of her tiny, pudgy hands. Maggie waited until she popped the triangle block into the right hole. She smiled and looked up to her mother for assurance.

Maggie squeezed Stuart's hand and stood up from her chair, walking over to the children.

"You did it, Faith! That's my girl. Mommy is so proud of you."

Little Faith. Faith Ollweyes. Smooth skin – the color of a hazelnut, shiny black ringlets forming on her head and a happy smile her birth mother would have given anything to see.

Maggie picked her daughter up and took her to the window to watch the birds eat at the wooden feeder outside.

The simple act of the sparrows flapping their wings, pecking at sunflower seeds and perching up to the roof of the feeder was as exciting to Faith as any circus or parade could dare to be. The simple things, Maggie found, were the most important.

As Faith laughed and pointed out the window, Maggie thought about the years her and Samuel had tried to conceive a baby and the pain they had suffered. After so many years, it occurred to her that they had, *together*, succeeded.

It was true, God works in mysterious ways.

Finding Faith had been her destiny all along.

AUTHOR'S NOTE

Finding Faith is a novel that, in a roundabout way, has been in my heart for some time. I began writing it immediately after finishing my first novel, *Simpler Times*, two years ago. Though the warm, nostalgic feelings meant for readers of the series are also found in *Finding Faith*, it is a far different story. Writing the last pages of *Finding Faith* brought a certain healing I hadn't realized I needed.

I hope that you, the reader, enjoyed the story and perhaps found hope or comfort within the pages.

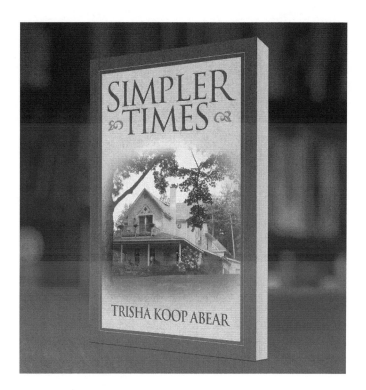

Rose loved visiting small rural towns as a child when her parents took her on road trips across Minnesota. Though she lived in a city growing up, she couldn't shake the fantasy of moving to a similar town like those she had vacationed at and opening her own little Inn.

At the young age of twenty-one her new husband wants to help make her dream come true and the couple makes plans to do just that. As luck may have it, Flynn, a US Army soldier, receives the call they both have dreaded. He is being deployed to Afghanistan for twelve months.

Left behind and distraught, paralyzed with worry, Rose feels she can take no more.

After headlines of war continue to cover the screen of her television one night, she grabs her car keys convinced a long drive out of the city may help clear her mind. Where the drive takes her is to an unexpected, quaint, very special town. There she meets newfound friends, realized dreams and a simpler life she yearns to have for her and Flynn.

But is it all too good to be true? Can it be snatched away as easily as it came about? And can the bond between Rose and Flynn surpass all understanding?

Made in the USA
Monee, IL
22 November 2024

70910193R00142